Vinod Bhardwaj is an art a̶̶̶̶̶̶̶̶̶̶̶̶̶̶̶̶ ....er. He has published two collectio̶̶̶̶ ̶̶y (*Jalta Makan* and *Hoshiarpur*), one short-story collection (*Chiteri*), and more than ten books on art and cinema. He has also compiled and published an acclaimed encyclopaedia of modern art in Hindi. This is his first novel in a trilogy. The second novel, *Sachcha Jhooth* (Truthful Lies) has already been published earlier this year.

Brij Sharma has worked with *The Times of India* and *Khaleej Times* of Dubai and has been Editor of *The Indian Express* in Gujarat. He has also translated into English Vinod Bhardwaj's Hindi monographs on artist Paramjit Singh and sculptor Ramesh Bisht and translated and contributed to the Dhoomimal Art Gallery book on F. N. Souza edited by him.

VINOD BHARDWAJ
TRANSLATED BY BRIJ SHARMA

SEPPUKU

THE CURIOUS WORKINGS OF THE ART MAFIA

HARPER PERENNIAL

NEW YORK • LONDON • TORONTO • SYDNEY • NEW DELHI

HARPER PERENNIAL

First published in English in 2015 by Harper Perennial
An imprint of HarperCollins *Publishers*

Originally published in Hindi in 2014 by Vani Prakashan, New Delhi

Copyright © Vinod Bhardwaj 2015
Translation copyright © Brij Sharma 2015

P-ISBN: 978-93-5177-046-6
E-ISBN: 978-93-5177-047-3

2 4 6 8 10 9 7 5 3 1

Vinod Bhardwaj asserts the moral right
to be identified as the author of this work.

HarperCollins *Publishers*
A-75, Sector 57, Noida, Uttar Pradesh 201301, India
1 London Bridge Street, London, SE1 9GF, United Kingdom
Hazelton Lanes, 55 Avenue Road, Suite 2900, Toronto, Ontario M5R 3L2
and 1995 Markham Road, Scarborough, Ontario M1B 5M8, Canada
25 Ryde Road, Pymble, Sydney, NSW 2073, Australia
195 Broadway, New York, NY 10007, USA

Typeset in 12/15 Adobe Devanagari
by Jojy Philip, New Delhi

Printed and bound at
Thomson Press (India) Ltd.

To my close friend and writer
Uday Prakash and his wife Kumkum

'Seppuku' is a synonym for 'Harakiri'. The samurai (Japan's warriors in the feudal age, equivalent to the *kshatriya* class in India) considered protecting their honour as their greatest hallmark. They considered suicide preferable to submitting to an insult or humiliation and that's what the other classes in society expected of them too. The form of suicide was also quite well defined—'Hara' meaning 'belly' and 'Kiri' meaning 'to cut'. They would rip their stomach with a dagger or knife. If that didn't kill them, they would summon another samurai to behead them. In the modern times, even the non-samurai took to seppuku. In the World War II, many soldiers in a vanquished army would choose seppuku over surrender. When the war ended, many among the depressed populace, in their moment of helplessness, also took to seppuku in the name of their emperor. The great writer Yukio Mishima committed suicide publicly through seppuku in 1970. But the tradition no longer prevails.

Life is Beautiful

I absolutely loathe the so-called Page Three culture propagated by the Capital's leading newspapers. All the same, I do occasionally throw a glance at the faces on that page. Once, courtesy Pratap Narayan, I found myself standing next to a beautician (who was trying to promote herself as a cosmetologist). And there I was the next day, staring out of the *Times of India*'s Page Three. That day, the phone did not stop ringing—my friends cursed and abused me until I was sick of it. 'So, you idiot, you too have finally graced Page Three!' But a couple of neighbours looked happy to see me while I was out on my morning walk. Some of them even greeted me. I was so embarrassed that I had to give up walking for a few days.

This morning too I threw a cursory, and shall I say deprecatory, glance at the wan and boring pictures on Page Three. Since Pratap Narayan's admission to hospital after he slipped into a coma, I had become indifferent to Page Three. Today was his seventh day in the coma. Yet here was a picture of him all smiles, a society beauty on his

1

arm, a glass of red wine in his hand. He was partial to rum (preferably Old Monk), but he had to drink red wine at parties. The art parties had recently stopped serving rum. It was fashionable to serve wine and cheese, or Scotch and samosas (Delhi's cultural contribution to such gatherings) at high-end parties.

I was not too surprised when I saw the photo. The caption merely said: 'Well-known painter Pratap Narayan with a model at a French Embassy party.' Son of a bitch. It was on his return from this very party that the worst chapter of his life had begun. He had bought a rupees 42-lakh limo just four days ago. 'If Husain saheb can go for a seven-crore Bugatti in London, then the world should know that my stream of piss too has length and force.'

I heard all of this from Trishna Art's Managing Director, Mrs Alka. Actually, I had ceased to be on talking terms with Pratap Narayan since 2008. With the crash of the European banks, the Indian art market had gone into a spin. By January 2010, it was teetering on the edge. But A-class painters like Pratap Narayan were safe—for now. Unfortunately, that very month, he went into a coma while returning home from the French party. He was in the driver's seat; the chauffeur was sitting in the back. All of a sudden, he complained of being sick. The confused chauffeur phoned Mrs Alka. Pratap Narayan had to be admitted to a hospital, where in just a matter of days, he went into a coma.

But 'bad news' had no meaning for Page Three editors. They weren't even aware that our star artist was lying in a coma, fighting for his life. Mrs Alka contributed to this confusion, since she had suppressed the news of his condition for quite a few days. She had been handling Pratap Narayan's image management and marketing for the last five years. So much so that Pratap would avoid his old-time friends if she was around. Once, at a five-star party at the Oberoi Hotel, she even gave him a tongue-lashing in front of us. 'P.N., stop this. The new German Ambassador's been looking for you, but you will lose a golden chance if you hang around with your bottle buddies.'

'Sorry, Alka...' And off went Pratap, spurred on by the rebuke.

In those days, if an old buddy (and I counted myself among them) phoned him to suggest spending an evening together, he would flatly refuse. Alka was dead against the rum culture and Pratap didn't care much for red wine, but for the past few years, he had taken to drinking red wine at grand parties more like a medicine. And he was forced to wear a smile, glass of red wine in hand, when facing Page Three photographers. Only when Alka was out of town would Pratap sometimes organize one of those rum parties in remembrance of the days gone past and down a peg or two. At one such rare party, he became so emotional that he began to sob. We were stunned. He was actually crying.

It seemed that Pratap no longer had any existence without Alka. He was there only when she was there. Like that café manager in Sartre's novel, *Nausea*, who feels empty within when the café is deserted. No wonder that at those rare rum parties Pratap's existential philosophy made him emotional. 'Do you recall that character in Camus' *The Plague*, who waits in the queue for hours, only to leave it just when his turn is about to come? I am that character.'

But once Alka returned to Delhi by the next morning's flight, Pratap's existential philosophy would go up in smoke. If any of us phoned him, he'd say: 'Why don't you come down for breakfast and have some alooparathas?'

Thus, he would spend his evenings at champagne-and-caviar parties in the company of society beauties, and his mornings with bottle-buddies and losers hogging alooparathas.

I had landed in Delhi from Bareilly in 1980, Pratap from Gorakhpur two years later. Full name: Pratap Narayan Rastogi. Diploma in Art from Lucknow University. My diploma, from the same university, was in Fine Arts. All my female classmates used to swoon over me.

Soon after my arrival in Delhi, I went to London for a year on a British Council scholarship. One day, I bought a picture postcard in Van Gogh's *Sunflowers* series from the National Gallery and posted it to Pratap with this message: 'Dear Pratap, miss you.'

Van Gogh was our idol in our youth. I remember an evening on a 'dry' day. I cannot recall how many cups of tea we had swigged, and till four in the morning had continued to debate and discuss Van Gogh's painting, whose story is linked to his attempt to lop off his ear and offer it to a streetwalker.

I was sure that Bareilly, a backwater when it came to modern art, would throw up the first artist to match a Picasso or a Souza. However, in the art world, no one knows the talented Baldev Sharma today. But Pratap Narayan Rastogi of Gorakhpur is thrust forward as the 'next Husain'. Husain and Pratap Narayan have only one thing in common.

Husain Saheb once told me: 'In my early years in the world of art, I would sit silent and speechless in the company of my friends, because I was not as fluent as them in English.' Pratap Narayan too would sit silent at get-togethers for his lack of command over the English language. He had not improved a bit. But now, he had incredible self-confidence. When your paintings begin to sell for millions, then girls, gallery managers, the rich and famous of this universe, and self-confidence insinuate themselves into your life, as if it were a package deal.

I am trying to recall Pratap's first trip to Bombay, where the young butterflies hired by the galleries were pulling all stops to lay hands on his canvases. We had put up our paintings at the studio and were waiting for buyers, when a butterfly from Gallerie Exit dragged Pratap away to a dance party. There, while dancing, she lifted her T-shirt for a second and asked him to look at the colour of her bra. 'Look, Pratap, look... Life is beautiful.' She wanted Pratap's works. Another buyer landed at the gallery carrying two bags of six million each in cash. 'Madam, I want two of Pratap's paintings at any cost.'

Some juicy tales of Pratap's unbelievable rise have become part of the art world's folklore. My favourite is his tiff with the middle-aged art critic, Kumud Kumari. Until some years ago, everyone in the art world was afraid of Kumud Kumari. Her pen wielded power and on her recommendation, even a nobody of an artist could go abroad on a scholarship. She must have been in her fifties at the time. She had a young daughter and her husband was a successful and busy director of a leading company. Kumud Kumari's evenings would be entirely dedicated to the world of art and culture. So much so that some wags claimed she had no time for dinner at home. Ever. Parties, parties, parties. Life is beautiful…or dutiful?

Pratap had a highly talented friend, a poet, who liked to down one peg too many. One evening, everyone downed more than his or her fill at a five-star hotel party. Pratap and his friend, Prakash (Prakash Shankar Mishra 'Prakash') asked for a lift in Kumud Kumari's limo for part of the way. She was driving herself. She liked wine, but watched her intake. Prakash was sitting in the back, floating on wings that the fourth peg will give you. From time to time, he would caress her cheeks, stroke her hair, and declare, 'I love you, Miss Kumud Kumari.'

But Kumud Kumari had spent the entire evening working on Pratap (many a time—opportunity permitting—pressing his leg) while the effusive display of gratitude was being made by the third wheel, i.e. Prakash. She told Pratap as much: 'Looks like Prakashji is in an expansive mood. Why don't you take a cue from him?'

'Well, I get quite disciplined after a drink. But don't you worry; I'll go down on my knees and open my heart to you one day after tea and samosas.'

'All right, I'll wait for that day.'

When that day arrived, Kumud Kumari was swept off her feet. There was this high tea at an embassy at five in the evening on the occasion of some exhibition. The skies suddenly became cloudy and the weather turned suitably romantic. Kumud Kumari, bubbling with joy, almost embraced Pratap when she ran into him. 'Oh ho, young man, such weather makes me heady!'

Pratap became quite serious and said to her: 'Then tell me, what's the colour...'

'Oh no, leave this arty talk. No discussion of Matisse's red in this weather.'

'Madam, I am not talking about the colours of art. What I want to know is the colour of your undies.'

Kumud Kumari looked closely at this small-town artist, who had migrated to a metro with dreams in his eyes, and burst out laughing. 'Looks like the high tea has sent you floating up in the air.'

'That's not the answer to my question.'

Kumud Kumari burst into another guffaw. 'Mister Pratap Narayan Rastogi, only a foolish woman would choose to wear undies in this weather.'

Pratap liked the riposte. Kumud Kumari had her flirtatious style. But even she was unable to foresee the attack that was to follow the high tea.

That evening, Pratap again took a lift in Kumud Kumari's limo. The conversation that day swung in the direction of British art critic and novelist John Berger's work *Permanent Red*. There was a deserted stretch just before the bus stop where Kumud Kumari was to drop Pratap. A shortcut. Vehicles rarely passed that way.

Once the car reached that stretch, Pratap abruptly stopped in the middle of a deep discussion and said: 'Mrs Kumud Kumari, please stop the car on the side.'

Kumud Kumari stopped. 'Young man, please relieve yourself a little way behind.'

'Madam...'

'Don't call me madam...I am not your madam.'

'Okay, Kumudji, I mean to do something else. I don't relieve myself by the roadside. V.S. Naipaul might get offended.'

'Then why did you ask me to stop the car?'

'I want you to just do what I say.'

And Pratap rattled off without any hitch or hesitation: 'Please unbutton your blouse for a while.'

Kumud Kumari, almost in a trance, followed his order. She said nothing and Pratap did nothing. Sitting in silence, he merely recalled a sketch by D.H. Lawrence of a naked woman sitting under a fruit tree. He had seen the work many years before and its memory had somewhat blurred. Then Kumud Kumari slowly buttoned up her blouse and started the car.

'See, I am not drunk. I am all right. I can still discuss John Berger,' Pratap said with a mischievous smile.

But Kumud Kumari remained silent and dropped Pratap at the bus stop.

The following day, the cultural attaché at the French Embassy phoned him. A young artist was to be sent to Paris for a six-month stint. Kumud Kumari had suggested Pratap's name.

Pratap phoned Kumud Kumari to thank her. But she was no longer in her informal mood. The 'Oh ho' style was gone. 'Look, you must visit the Rodin Museum in Paris. There, you'll find everybody crowding around *The Thinker*. But you must spend some quality time looking at a small sculpture called *The Fatigue*. You will want to return to it time and again and one day you will discover that your own fatigue has gone. That will be the moment of truth for the artist in you.'

Before he left for Paris, Kumud Kumari invited Pratap to a classical concert. Her daughter was also there. Pratap was cool with it. After the 'dose' of high tea, he realized that Kumud Kumari didn't want to take any further risks. She must have thought that this boy was more dangerous when not drunk.

Pratap wore sandals to the concert, which he had taken off while seated. As he listened to the singer, he began to rhythmically tap his bare feet in tandem with her voice. Soon, Kumud Kumari's bare foot began to rub against his leg. Pratap was scared. He had this feeling that Kumud's daughter, Sadhana Kumari, was watching. What would she make of it?

Pratap came out of the hall . He badly wanted to go to Paris. In a Godard film, some characters are shown running across the Louvre Museum. Pratap loved this idea. This thought of racing across Paris's great museum.

This was his last adventure with Kumud Kumari. Once he became the Page Three hero, he had a different kind of adventure with Sadhana Kumari, Kumud Kumari's only daughter, who had perhaps noticed—or maybe not— something in the semi-darkness of that evening's concert. We will obviously discuss this adventure with a difference a little later.

Right now, I am feeling strangely feverish. I have been googling for details of the state of coma. Normally, a man lapses into a coma for no more than two to three weeks. It is also possible for him to miraculously wake up from it. In the history of medicine, the record for remaining in coma is 42 years.

At a meeting organized by the Gorakhpur-based art-cultural outfit Aarambh, Pratap had read out parts of Sartre's *Nausea*. In my bout of fever I could hear him read out:

'At the age of thirty I feel sorry for myself. There are times when I wonder if I wouldn't do best to spend in one year the three hundred thousand francs I have left—and afterwards... But what would that give me? New suits? Women? Travel? I've had all that, and now it's over, I don't feel like it anymore: not for what I'd get out of it! A year from now I'd find myself as empty as I am today, without even a memory and afraid to face death.'

Ignoring whatever happened between us, I am thinking about Pratap lying in a coma. There is a flood of memories.

Down at the reception, the owner of New Art Gallery Mrs Pratibha Bansal is in the middle of an argument about carrying a bouquet up to Pratap. The receptionist tells her: 'Madam, you can't carry flowers up to the patient. There is a danger of infection.' Mrs Bansal looks at me, thrusts the bouquet into my hands, and right then, decides to tell someone on the phone: 'I can't sell the painting right now. You see, its price is going to go up. There's only a slim chance of his coming out of the coma.'

I walk out of the hospital and throw the bouquet in a garbage dump. The auto driver is reluctant to go by the meter. I feel like a man possessed and begin to shout at him like a deranged being. He is alarmed and confused and quickly agrees to go by the meter. After many attempts, he manages to start the auto. He throws a glance at me, wondering whether the bearded fakir has escaped from a madhouse. 'Sorry, sir, I saw you on TV last night.'

Art Seppuku

Speaking of a person lying in a coma, it is believed that it's well nigh impossible to conjecture about the likelihood of his recovery. Everybody's story of how they lapsed into a coma is unique. Moreover, if a person continues to remain in a coma for a very long time, his chances of revival tend to reduce. All the same, some comatose people do wake up even after a lapse of many weeks, though physically, they might feel drained and inadequate. Indeed, lapsing into a coma is nothing but losing consciousness to the point of no return. The person is completely oblivious of all activity around them, and one might have a false impression that the comatose person is in a deep slumber. But no amount of even painful prodding revives them. The person just doesn't react to his surroundings.

While I hadn't been in touch with Pratap for many months, and in the course of a debate on a well-known TV channel, had raised some disturbing questions about his success story, after watching him lying in a coma in the hospital, I honestly wished him recovery. In the days when we had been close friends, I had twice watched him escape the jaws of death. Why should he be denied a third chance?

The TV debate was another story. The channel had phoned me in the hope of obtaining the name of some artist or art critic who would be willing to speak out against M.F. Husain. 'We are looking for a good speaker, who would come down on Husain Saheb for his misdeeds…'

'Why? What has he done? You drove him out, you sent him into exile, but it appears that hasn't satisfied you…'

'You see, Aishwarya Rai and Abhishek Bachchan are getting engaged this evening. And sitting in Dubai, Husain Saheb drew a cartoon, which has already been published in a newspaper, showing the bride and groom on a horse while Salman Khan sits by the roadside holding an empty begging bowl. How do you justify the timing of the cartoon?'

'You people have absolutely no sense of humour. Husain Saheb knows the art of keeping himself in the headlines, but your channel seems to have nothing much to offer. Since you are barred from Amitabh Bachchan's bungalow, you are using Husain Saheb's sketch to launch an empty debate. If you want to attack art, why don't you attack Pratap Narayan Rastogi? He is currently a rage in Europe. Even Husain Saheb was never embraced by the European art market in this fashion. Tell me, what's so great about Pratap Narayan that all the big-time collectors there should be falling for him head over heels?'

The channel didn't invite me that evening, but after a few days they did phone me to join in a debate on Pratap Narayan's success story. I was, in any case, bitterly against him, so I went all out to question and criticize his unbelievable success.

Pratap hadn't watched the show, but there was no dearth of cronies who would report to him. And they promptly conveyed it to him, all spiced up and exaggerated. Predictably, an hour before midnight, Pratap called. 'I hear you were running me down on TV. Why do you have a grudge against me? Are you jealous of my wealth or the number of girlfriends I have or my fame? What's your problem?'

'Pratap, I remember when we were close friends and shared rooms for four years. Obviously, we were privy to each other's secrets. But on the programme I had raised some serious questions about the art market today. You were not the focus of the debate. The Indian art market was the real issue—it has crossed the limits of sanity. Your success is merely a symbol of that malaise, a pointer, a sort of metaphor...'

'If this market hasn't helped you to improve your lot, why do you have to vent your frustration in this fashion?'

'Pratap, have you heard the expression "corporate seppuku"?'

'Now what's this new term you have coined? What has the art market to do with this "corporate seppuku"?'

'I'm sure you know the Japanese word hara-kiri. There was a time when you used to talk a lot about hara-kiri. But the real word is seppuku. When a samurai or a Japanese warrior slits his stomach to commit suicide, it's called seppuku. These days, the Indian art market is witnessing this very phenomenon—art seppuku...'

I heard Pratap hooting with laughter. 'My dear Baldev, it's a nice word. And has a musical lilt...'

'Look, Pratap, when a samurai is compelled to take the

difficult road to seppuku, he follows the ritual of suicide like a fine art. He commits suicide only when he either wants to escape the ignominy of becoming his adversary's prisoner or when he has committed a despicable deed. In the course of a war, a samurai is unable to observe all the complex rituals of his vocation. But seppuku committed by a true samurai has an entire compendium of rituals attached to it. There is something unique and formal about it. A samurai has to don white apparel, he has to visit a Buddhist temple and compose a poem before committing suicide. And the latter calls for the observance of its own etiquette. Thus, he is not allowed to compose a poem about his own demise...'

'It's certainly interesting. But what's the relevance of this warrior to the art market?'

'You see, Pratap, while the art market doesn't have a samurai's book of forms, rituals, ethics, discipline, and craft, its constituents occasionally do commit hara-kiri. Consider this: Two years ago, Trishna Gallery was unable to sell a four-by-four-foot painting of Ramesh Mehrotra's even for 50,000 rupees. But once the art market's sales figures rose beyond proportion and bank officials began to go around carrying graphs of the artists' magical success, similar work by him began to sell for eight lakhs. Why, one day, I got a call from the desperate owner of a small gallery: 'Baldevji, the prices of Ramesh's canvases have set the art market on fire. It's impossible to get hold of even one for eight lakhs. What do I do?'

'But finally, Ramesh was exposed. Today, nobody wants his paintings even for two lakhs. That's art seppuku. And that's what I want you to understand. I would advise you to keep an eye on those who were desperate to acquire your work, towing stroller bags filled with 60 lakhs in cash, and watch where they end up. This virus of seppuku is spreading across the world of art like a plague. Indeed, the art market is full of terrible scenarios resulting from mass seppuku. The fearful glow of a nuclear war is lighting up the skies and all the warriors are being compelled to commit seppuku.'

'What you've told me certainly makes sense. But I can also make out an element of jealousy; why didn't a gallery queen dragging a stroller of cash knock at your door when the art market was at its peak? Don't forget that when the first of those bags landed at my studio, you were part of the celebration and were busy downing pegs of Blue Label Scotch. The truth is that the high and mighty of the art market who committed seppuku publicly, have gone to heaven after their demise. Look at that guy who worked as a salesman on a peon's salary at Parvati Art Gallery until a few years ago. Today, he is the owner of a huge apartment in a posh colony and cruises around in an air-conditioned limo.'

'Then you might also know that nowadays he doesn't invest in art, but is looking for deals in the property market. The Western art market is no cleaner. But what has happened and is happening in India has no parallel. Can you fathom the pain of that young artist, who within six months of his arrival in Delhi from Barabanki, found that the prices of his canvases had shot up from 50,000 rupees to two lakhs? And now that nobody wants to touch his work, he has become a psychological wreck. I am afraid he might commit suicide any day.'

'Come on, you are a scaremonger. Come to my studio tomorrow. Even a dead elephant is worth a lakh and a quarter, as they say. I'll serve you genuine Blue Label.'

That was our last conversation. It's true that even during the bad times of art seppuku, Pratap didn't face any problems. Indeed, he remained busy throwing parties and slept soundly. It was down-in-the-dumps people like us who had to spend sleepless nights crying.

I have become really emotional, as I look at Pratap lying in a coma. I remember the afternoon he'd gone to Chanakya Cinema to watch James Bond's *Die Another Day*. We shared quarters in those days. I had no interest in Bond movies. How could a dedicated fan of Ingmar Bergman enjoy Bond?

Around three in the afternoon, Pratap called me: 'Baldev, I am in very bad shape. Come to the Chanakya toilet quickly. I have locked myself in and am lying on the floor, soaked in blood.'

He sounded like he was in acute pain. I rushed to Chanakya on my motorcycle. He was lying prone on the floor, his kurta soaked in blood.

While watching the movie, suddenly, he had discovered something dripping from his left nostril. Initially, he couldn't figure out what it was. With his characteristic sense of humour, he rationalized that James Bond had punched him. But soon after, he was compelled to leave the hall. His nose was bleeding like a tap. He ran for the toilet, writhing in excruciating pain, and lay down on the floor. There was no stopping the blood. For a moment, he thought: 'Pratap, your end is nigh. You had this dream that you would leave the world while creating a painting. But you are destined to die a bizarre death. James Bond extended his fist out of the screen, punched you and you left this world.'

I took Pratap to a nursing home. His blood pressure had shot up. A Malayali nurse bandaged his nose and gave him an injection. After five hours of bed rest, Pratap decided to attend a cocktail party. I was surprised to see him there. As soon as he arrived, he sought out Sadhana Kumari and started out by praising her dress. I noticed he also winked at me.

Two years down the line, Pratap had to again face a similar situation. This time around, he was at home. He had been painting all night and had gone to bed very late. In the morning, while he was brushing his teeth, his nose began to bleed. He screamed down the phone at me: 'Baldev, take me to a hospital! And if the bleeding doesn't stop, then do me a favour and just throttle me!'

I was quite harried. Somehow, I got Pratap admitted to a hospital. He had to spend a night there—the first time he had spent a night in a hospital. When I visited him the next morning, he was lying in bed, all smiles, listening to Beethoven's Ninth Symphony on his system. 'Ballubhai, I am all right now. The Ninth always revives me. What joy...'

'Then shall I throttle you now? This is the right moment...'

'No, no. As of now, let's talk only about love, about sex, what the hell! When the nurse was busy with my ECG yesterday, her massive breasts brushed against me every now and then, pushing me back towards the river of life. I was moving away from Thanatos towards Eros... You know the Greek names, don't you? Once you are out of the bloody clutches of the god of death, the soft embraces of the goddess of love feel so pleasurable.'

'So you are back in form.'

The doctor was a young Bengali lady. She advised Pratap to go on an hour's brisk walk every day and also suggested a diet regime. I was there when Pratap asked her out of the blue: 'And what about sex? Do I have to stay away from it?'

The doctor smiled. 'No, Mister Artist, how would you paint otherwise? Tolstoy couldn't write without it, Picasso couldn't paint without it...'

'Oh, you are quite well-informed, well-read.'

Pratap looked after himself for a couple of days. He would go for the regulation morning walk, and on his return, he would come up with comments in his familiar juicy vein. 'Baldev, when I notice some women walking ahead of me swinging their butts, I don't feel like overtaking them.'

Four days after he had left the hospital, I got a call from him in the afternoon. I'd been sitting in Divya Art Gallery, waiting for the owner since ten in the morning. The bank had returned her cheque.

'Baldev, do me a favour,' he said.

'What is it now?'

'Guess what?'

'Pratap, tell me quickly. I am in a bad mood. Mrs Makhija hasn't arrived at her gallery yet and I am getting bored sitting amidst third-rate paintings.'

'Do one thing: spend the evening at Volga Restaurant drinking beer. The treat is on me. I'll pay the bill in cash as soon as we meet.'

'What's happened? Are you off to Paris or London on some new scholarship? You sound quite chirpy.'

'The news is sweeter. Sadhana Kumari phoned me. She is

coming. She's definitely coming this time, after ditching me four times in a row.'

'Did you tell her about your moments of joy during your trip to the hospital?'

'You are stupid. A young and sexy girl wants to come to my house. I have already dropped her discreet hints. She is very happy. And you want me to tell her about my hospital experiences. Don't forget that the doctor didn't bar me from having sex…'

'Look, if you become a martyr, I am not going to carry your body to the burning ground.'

'The electric crematorium will do!' Pratap hooted. 'My only request is, please come home a little late. Today is an auspicious beginning. This day has come after overcoming many hurdles.'

I spent the evening alone at Volga, recalling Nirmal Verma's story 'Lovers'. *The shaft of sunlight hid under the piano like a rabbit*…etc. etc. And Pratap Narayan Rastogi was busy dallying with the only daughter of the capital's most eminent critic of art and culture.

This time, 'lucky' Pratap got a long-term scholarship from the British Council. And Sadhana Kumari promised to accompany him to see Henry Moore's sculptures.

Pratap's comment was worth noting: 'I find Henry Moore's drawings more powerful. You come to see Francis Bacon's paintings with me. He is the real face of modern art.'

A few years later, Pratap had forgotten all about Bacon and was singing paeans to Damien Hirst. He now dreamt of becoming India's Damien Hirst.

'Why don't you become India's Pratap Narayan Rastogi?'

'Come on, don't be silly! Call me PNR. That's how I should be known in the world of art.'

The Indian art world had not been afflicted by the curse of seppuku yet.

The Kissing Queen and Her Slap

I think the year was 1983. One day, I learnt that artist F.N. Souza was in town. He lived in New York, but had lately been visiting India quite frequently, sometimes to hold his exhibitions. I decided to go to one of his shows at Dhoomimal Gallery in Connaught Place. In those days, we lived in awe of the leading Delhi art galleries. When I arrived there, I found Ravi Jain, one of the owners, sitting with Souza. A little mound of samosa lay in the centre of the table. Ravi Jain asked me: 'Are you an artist?'

'Yes,' I said politely, which prompted him to invite me to join them: 'Have some samosas. All the famous artists of India have enjoyed them sitting at this table.'

I picked up one somewhat hesitantly. Actually, I was dying to talk to Souza, but as usual, discovered that I was incapable of expressing myself coherently on account of my fractured English. Souza looked at my sketchbook and was kind enough to praise me in glowing terms. And when I asked him to make a sketch for me, he readily agreed and even asked me: 'Shall I make your sketch?'

At this point, an art critic walked in, carrying a dozen or so newspapers and flaunting a row of nearly an equal number of pens in his front pocket. Souza quickly drew a sketch of him, signed the result and handed it to me. I wanted to meet Souza once more, with Pratap in attendance. I noted down his hotel address and he told me to come down at 5:00 pm the following day.

Pratap was equally keen to meet Souza. In the warrens of Daryaganj was a hotel-like building called Jeevan Guest House. That's where Souza often stayed when in Delhi. Pratap and I were intrigued that one of India's leading painters camped out in that ramshackle hotel.

Our dialogue with Souza obviously progressed in broken English. While conversing, I somehow found courage to ask Souza: 'Sir, do you follow Hindi? Are you able to speak a little bit of it?'

Souza, never lost for words when answering such questions, said: 'Yes, I know enough Hindi to find my way around G.B. Road.'

Pratap couldn't help laughing. '*Wah*, Souza Saheb! We're really impressed! What a straight and clear-cut answer!'

Pratap and I had been to G.B. Road once. We had heard that up and coming artists often frequented such neighbourhoods in search of inspiration.

Just then, Souza got a phone call from a gallery owner. We could hear him tell the woman at the other end: 'See, I cannot do anything about it. Yes, you are right when you say that by under-selling me, these women often spoil my market. But they aren't professional gallery owners. And please also try to understand my problem. What these women give me in return for my paintings is essential to my existence. To hell with the art market!'

I motioned to Pratap that it was time to leave, when there was a knock at the door. There stood a lovely young thing, her hair in a tousle. Souza must have an appointment with her, I guessed. It was time for us to disappear.

Once we emerged on the road, Pratap said: 'Baldev, whatever you say, here's an extraordinary man! There was a time when the London art world adored him. But did you notice how naturally he has adjusted himself to living in a seedy hotel in this Daryaganj lane?'

'If you ask me, Souza would get hardly any inspiration sitting in a hotel like the Taj. Did you notice how easily he gives away his drawings? And here we have our small-time Delhi artists, who would lend you one drawing for a magazine and then remind you ten times in a day that it was time they had it back, as if some desperate buyer was waiting to grab it.'

Souza had told us that when he visited art critic Richard Bartholomew's house, he was shocked to discover there were hardly any works of art on the walls. And said: 'It's impossible for an art critic in the west to not be surrounded by works received as gifts.'

Pratap had been invited by a well-known art collector that evening. There were dozens of stories doing the rounds of the Delhi art circuit about him. That he drank a lot; he was a bachelor, so if you landed up at his place in the evening, you would be lucky to escape before 11; sometimes, one had to hang around till four in the morning; he had an eye for art; he had picked up the works of many leading artists on the cheap at the right time and now it was a pot of gold that helped him to maintain his lifestyle. The prices of works he had bought towards the end of the 1990s had truly reached the skies. He now hawked for three million rupees what he may have bought for 60,000.

Pratap asked me: 'Why don't you come along? He has bought a drawing from me and I have to collect the payment.'

When we arrived there, we found Nandlal Bhatia sitting in his vast drawing-room. He had a can of Coca-Cola in front of him and was sipping a cocktail of vodka and Coke. Pratap introduced me and the conversation took off on a very congenial note. On our arrival, Nandlal had immediately handed Pratap 2,000 rupees in cash for his drawing. Both of us opted for beer. Nandlal now set out to show us his collection. He had works of nearly all the major artists.

After sundown, Nandlal took out a bottle of whisky. We had thought he'd produce some expensive Scotch, but it was merely Solan No. 1. All the same, we enjoyed Nandlal's monologue. Every now and then, he'd place his hand on my shoulder as he showed a piece of work. At one point, we were discussing a particular painting, when he disappeared into his rooms for about 25 minutes to look for it. On his return, painting in hand, he looked at his watch and exclaimed: 'It has taken me exactly 22 minutes and 33 seconds to fish out this Jamini Roy.'

We were bowled over by Nandlal's sense of precision. He laughed: 'Look, some years ago, I read a long interview of Gabriel Garcia Marquez in the *Paris Review*, where he had impressed upon the interviewer the significance of exact figures. His argument was that if you claimed that elephants were flying in the sky, nobody was going to believe you. But if you claimed that 787 elephants were flying, then people might take you at your word; the claim would appear to be a fact to them.'

By 9 o'clock, Nandlal had emptied Solan No. 1. Now it was the turn of white wine and he promptly produced a bottle of French wine from his bar. He took out some crystal glasses and we set about enjoying the expensive wine.

While we were in our cups, a Western lady, claiming to be a connoisseur of art, walked in. We prepared to leave, but Nandlal stopped us: 'No, no. You can't. You must have dinner now.'

Pratap was swaying because of the cocktail of beer and wine. I was unsteady too, but noticed that Pratap had his gaze fixed on the woman. Suddenly, he turned romantic: 'The lines on your forehead tell me a very interesting story.'

'Then tell me that story...' she responded with a coy smile. Pratap appeared to be in a mood to seduce her. But before he could come out with a choice cocktail of spiritual-intellectual verbiage, I heard Nandlal scream: 'Nonsense! It's all nonsense!'

The outburst stunned Pratap. What had happened to this man? Initially, the argument was confined to words, but soon both of them stood up and started pushing each other. That lovely evening was doomed to end on a tragic note. Nandlal chased Pratap right up to the lift, nearly hitting him in the process. I did try to intervene, but Nandlal, mad with rage, was beyond controlling. Somehow, we managed to escape and emerged on the street in one piece. A beautiful evening had dissolved into a bad dream.

We had hardly started to walk, when Pratap stopped in his tracks. 'Let's go back to that bastard. Let's give him a thrashing and puncture his balloon of being an art collector. Did the bastard buy me with the 2,000 rupees?'

'Come on now, let's go home. He's a lean and scrawny guy. If you hit him, he might collapse. And the headlines tomorrow will scream: "Drunken artist kills defenceless art collector".'

Pratap looked at his watch. 'We'll press his bell at exactly 13 minutes past 11 and then give him exactly 13 slaps. The bastard will forget Marquez!'

That evening, or night, had now entered a surrealist phase. I also began to laugh and fortified with liquid courage, we walked back to Nandlal's flat and pressed the doorbell. Nandlal opened the door and Pratap immediately told him the exact time. 'It's 13 minutes and 23 seconds past 11. And now you need just one tight one on the ears.'

By then, Nandlal had nearly forgotten about the scuffle. Pratap gave him a sharp slap, and instead of taking the lift, ran down the stairs, followed by me. Downstairs, the guard couldn't figure out what had hit the saheb's guests.

In any case, the slap did not cost Pratap much. Many years later, when Pratap's market graph was on the rise at breakneck speed, Nandlal showed up at his studio with a bag full of 1,000-rupee notes. When Pratap's PA informed him, he ensured that Nandlal cooled his heels in the lobby for two hours. In the meantime, he quietly left through another exit, while Nandlal continued to wait for him in vain.

The story of the slap, which Pratap administered to Sadhana Kumari is more tragic. During the days when they were besotted lovers, I was often an unwilling listener to the endless graphic narratives of the goings-on between them. Pratap used to call her Kissing Queen in those days and they actually appeared to spend hours kissing and cuddling up to each other, secure in the secluded arbours of Lodi Gardens. Why, they had tested their ardour in every corner of every domed monument there.

More than painting, Sadhana claimed to love poetry. She was a sort of poetaster herself. Those were the days when I frequented libraries to pick, choose and transcribe lines and stanzas from the collections of the finest poets and brought them to Pratap. Neruda, Brecht, Dylan Thomas… though Pratap was more interested in kisses than in poetry. In his cocoon of fantasy, he even kept count of the kisses and would sometimes throw bizarre morsels at me late at night: 'I managed to have 351 kisses under dome number three today. *Sadhana safal rahi* (my dedication paid off).'

Obviously, I was never part of any of this pleasure seeking. All the same, I was helpless and had to listen to all the graphic and minute details of their dalliance. I did enjoy them for a few days, but soon it got boring. Yet, there was no escaping the tall tales of their episodic romance. Quite often, Pratap added to the burden of my boredom by overwhelming me with the lifeless lines of Sadhana Kumari's attempts at cobbling together some poetry. In the morning, I'd hand him the finest of Neruda's lines, but my reward at night was to listen to Sadhana Kumari's Bollywoodian dross.

Pratap may have been born in Gorakhpur—and was not a child of the Internet generation—but he had an almost encyclopaedic knowledge of the most obscure art, cinema, literature, etc. Besides he was an expert at name-dropping to boot. He was not too proficient in English, but compensated for it with the treasure-trove of weighty and grandiloquent words he had at his command, which sometimes left even the highly educated city slickers stumped. For example, at an exhibition sometime in the 1980s, he ran into Mrs Kusum Jain and she bought one of his paintings. While getting into her luxury limo, she asked Pratap: 'Why don't you join me? You should also spend some time at spiritual discourses. I am off to Golf Links. My driver will drop you home later.'

Pratap tagged along. A Jain guru's lecture on spiritualism was in progress in a tiny hall on the terrace of a villa. Most of the wealthy women there, heads bent, were listening to him in complete silence, when they were distracted by the arrival of a bearded and long-haired young man in the company of Mrs Jain. Who was he, they wondered. Another guru?

Within 15 minutes, Pratap felt oppressed and left the hall. Someone had tried to create a semblance of greenery on the terrace. A few flower-pots held some lovely cacti. While Pratap considered them, he noticed a middle-aged woman near him. Finding a listener, she launched into a serious monologue on the search of the self. Pratap had just finished reading R.D. Laing's *The Divided Self*. On the basis of that book, he managed to hold his own. Soon, the woman was listening to him raptly.

That's when the sordid truth sunk into Pratap that while he had landed in the capital to make his name as a painter, he was heading towards becoming the spiritual guru of obscenely rich men's wives, who were drowning in the well of boredom. Pratap delved into his powerful vocabulary to fend off such thoughts, so he asked her: 'Well, have you ever heard of the word cunnilingus?'

'No, but it sounds musical. What does it mean?'

'It's a Greek word. I find cunnilingus a highly spiritual experience, where a man with nothing to hold, pays consummate homage to a woman's sacrosanct vagina. I believe cunnilingus is a form of art and is not everyone's cup of tea. Why don't you ask your husband to find the meaning and references to this word?'

The woman gaped at Pratap in silence for a while. Then said: 'You better give this advice to Kusumji. I don't like this dirty talk.' In high dudgeon, she hurried back to the discourse. Pratap went downstairs and told Kusum Jain's driver: 'Madam will take some time, so drop me at Khirki.'

But Kissing Queen Sadhana Kumari was taking full advantage of Pratap's expertise in the art of cunnilingus. And Pratap too exploited the liaison for quite a while. Gradually, Sadhana Kumari's mother began to realize that she might end up becoming Mrs Robinson. She, therefore, tried her best to help Pratap obtain a British Council scholarship and made unsparing efforts to make him the darling of the media.

One afternoon, Sadhana Kumari got so bored at a programme at the India International Centre that she decided to leave it half way and headed for the domes of Lodi Gardens to ruminate over her past. Once there, she chanced upon Pratap near her favourite monument in the company of a girl, who looked like a gargoyle, to put it mildly. Initially, she thought she was mistaken. But no, it was Pratap indeed. And look at his cheek! He was smooching that gargoyle!

Sadhana Kumari seethed with rage, but left the garden quietly; she was in no mood to create a scene. Next morning, she drove her huge limo into the narrow lanes of Khirki. As she rang the doorbell, I came face-to-face with her.

'Good morning, Sadhanaji. How nice to see you so early in the morning. My day is made.'

'Your day is certainly made, but your friend stands no chance today!'

She followed this up with the choicest of Hindi expletives, which sounded like unlikely slokas at that hour of the day. She was as foul-mouthed as a sweeper. If she had vented her rage in English it would have made little difference. But Sadhana Kumari mouthing chaste Hindi expletives?! Oh my God! Let Pratap put up with this alone. I somehow managed to escape, telling Sadhana Kumari that I was off on my morning walk. Pratap was wide awake by this time.

'Mister Pratap, if I am supposed to be *your* Kissing Queen, then who the hell was that fat buffalo you were smooching near my favourite dome in Lodi Gardens? The least I expect is for you to fall for someone attractive!'

Pratap tried to fend off the assault with some intellectual rigmarole. But Sadhana Kumari was determined to make full use of her handbook of Hindi expletives. Suddenly, she picked up a paperweight from the table. For a second, Pratap thought he was going to lose an eye. The stunningly beautiful Sadhana Kumari was mad with rage. Pratap thought the planting of a kiss would do the trick, but he was mistaken.

'Look, Sadhana, I'd met that girl as part of a Doordarshan programme on art. Kuber Dutt was interviewing me at the National Gallery of Modern Art, where she was assisting him. She even produced a comb out of her purse for me to arrange my hair.'

'So you had called her over to Lodi Gardens to give her back that comb? Is that it? And that too in front of the dome where you had kissed me for the first time? You bloody liar!'

Pratap felt there was only one way to contain Sadhana Kumari's rage. He planted a thick and heavy slap on her left cheek. 'Sadhana, please give peace a chance.'

Sadhana stopped in her tracks and looked at Pratap with her fiery eyes. She took a painting off the wall, flung it on the ground and began to stomp on it to deface and destroy it. (Subsequently Pratap used that painting, just as Sadhana Kumari had left it, as part of his notorious installation, 'The Last Slap'). Pratap realized that no further action was called for on his part.

'Sadhana, please, you may slap me too if you like. I won't feel bad. Come on. Give me a slap.'

'Slap you I will, but only when it suits me. Not here, where no one's watching.'

Thereafter, Sadhana Kumari disappeared from Pratap's life for 11 months. She would not even take his calls. For some time, she escaped to Florence, where she would sob, sitting opposite Michelangelo's *David*. (She told me this when she once ran into me by chance.)

All the same, the relationship between the Kissing Queen and the Cunnilingus King ended on a painful note. An art institution in the capital had awarded Pratap some prize. Just as Pratap was about to accept it, Sadhana Kumari made a dramatic appearance on the stage and landed a resounding slap on his face. Looking at the situation, Pratap mumbled, 'Thank you, Sadhana' and managed to control the damage to some extent.

And now, only this morning, someone phoned me to say that Sadhana Kumari had visited Pratap lying in a coma at the hospital, and had cried silently, standing by his bedside.

The Strange Tale of
Suhas Hande

An evening in 2006. It's raining heavily. The bell rings. It's a taxi driver, standing at the door, drenched. 'Sir, a man sitting in my cab wants to see you. He can't climb up the stairs.'

I rush downstairs, worried and intrigued. It's Suhas Hande. 'Sorry for disturbing you in this weather, Baldev. I had gone to Pratap Narayan's studio, but the guard at the gate insisted he was away at some party... I could make out, though, that he was very much there.'

'*Arre*, he is a very busy star now. He has no time for strugglers like us. After all, time is money.'

Suhas, a Page Three celebrity in his time, roused my pity, as he sat in the cab. He needed 1,500 rupees so he could pay off the cabbie and then have a square meal at some dhaba. Ever since he'd lost his left foot in an accident, fame, women and money had deserted him in quick succession. He had gone back from Delhi to Aurangabad to lend a hand in his brother's business, but had been turned away. He was back

33

in Delhi now to sell some of his old sculptures. But alas, even though the art market was on the rise, his graph was moving downhill.

By chance, I had some 2,500 rupees lying with me. I rushed back and took out 2,000 to hand to him. I didn't have the heart to see him in that condition. 'No, Baldev, just 1,500 will do. I know that even you are going through a tough time.'

But I forced the cash on him. This was our last meeting. Later, the very same evening, I came to know about his death (he had committed suicide near the caves of Ellora).

Right after Suhas's death, there was an opening of an exhibition followed by a cocktail party at Gallerie Dreamhouse, which also included his works.

Dreamhouse was located in a grand South Delhi mall. But to reach that godforsaken complex, one had to walk past the city's worst and most stinky garbage dump. I had seen that place clean and spruced up only once—in the year of the Surat plague, when the Delhi chief minister himself had launched a cleanliness drive in the city and was photographed flaunting a broom. Sushmita Sen had arrived in the capital wearing the Miss Universe crown to take part in her victory parade, but her arrival was heralded by a plague scare in the city.

I believe this metropolis needs to be perpetually under the threat of some plague-like scourge, so at least the stinking hell at the square between the five-star hospital and the palatial mall would stay clean!

On that evening, I found the stink rising from that dump even more loathsome. Time and again, I recalled Suhas Hande's face, sitting in the cab in the driving rain. I didn't expect much from Gallerie Dreamhouse, but it could have at least announced a two-minute silence in his memory.

While inaugurating the show, Dreamhouse owner Hema Gupta didn't even bring up Suhas' name, though I had discreetly briefed her about his suicide. She pretended to be taken aback, mechanically muttering, 'May God rest his soul in peace. A tragic end for an unfortunate artist,' etc., etc.

The cocktail party was in full swing with cheese and wine doing the rounds. Beautiful women were coming and going and gatecrashers were busy hogging the buffet and downing the free-flowing liquor. I complained to Hema: 'You should have at least announced a two-minute silence for Suhas. There was a time when you had brought out a large and lavish catalogue for his show and sold his works for thousands.'

'Mister Baldev, I can understand your sentiments. But this is not the time for grief... You see, life goes on. No one dies with the dead.'

At a time when Pratap was hardly able to make ends meet, Suhas Hande had been a Page Three hero.

As more and more money flowed into the art world, Delhi newspapers finally began to accept the importance of art parties on the social circuit. There was a time when the press would completely ignore art parties. But once works of art began to sell for crores at auctions on a weekly basis, this attitude changed and artists were ranked as being powerful in their own right. Some galleries even started the practice of paying to have their photographs published. The money initially went to the PROs, but soon enough, newspapers found ways to squeeze this cash directly.

One day, I ran into a photographer from my hometown. He was on Page Three duty for some big daily at a party organized by the Ministry of Foreign Affairs. He came up to me and almost complained: 'How come I don't see any celebrity here?'

'What about me? Bastard, why don't you take my picture?'

'You rascal, what will I do with your ragamuffin image? Have you considered this bag on your shoulder? Dump this bag on that chair and go and stand next to that lovely face, and I promise to take your photograph. The caption would be: "The Beauty and the Beast!"'

'Okay, if you want a celebrity, go and photograph that guy sitting with that Italian Odissi dancer. His name is Suhas Hande. He is a talented sculptor.'

Believe me, he walked up to them and actually clicked their image. Then gleefully returned to me: 'A really smart guy. After I'd taken the pic, he quietly thrust a 500-rupee note into my pocket.'

Once the photographer had left the party, I greeted Suhas: 'So, now you will be on Page Three.'

'Really?'

'Of course. That photographer is a friend. You should check the paper day after tomorrow.'

Apparently, because that day's paper had no ad on Page Three, Suhas and Gabriella's picture appeared in it spread across four columns. It was a big 'entry' for him. Those were the final years of the nineties. Money had not yet inundated the world of art, but was about to. The talk of the town was the imminent boom in the Indian art market.

To celebrate the photograph, Suhas threw a party for Pratap and me in a Defence Colony bar. Pratap considered his art retrograde, but he exploited that evening to the hilt.

From that day on, Suhas began to be counted among the celebrities. Some celebrities in the capital appeared to me rather pitiable, like party gatecrashers. They would arrive at a party dressed up to the nines and behave rather oddly. Some foreign ladies would float around in costumes meant solely to draw the photographers' eye. Some even flaunted large, specially designed colourful hats. And amid all this, the owner of one of the large galleries would always shoo the photographers away. I am not Page Three material, he'd declare.

Then there was Mr Agrawal, an art collector who, for some mysterious reason, tended to dominate every art party. He was 77 and, quite often, could be seen with a pipe dangling from his mouth. Once Suhas became an accepted member of the Page Three club, he would often stand with Mr Agrawal, ready with a 500-rupee note to thrust on the photographer. He learnt rather late in the day that Mr Agrawal kept a 1,000-rupee note ready for the very same purpose.

Those were the days when Pratap derided the Page Three culture. He would tell me: 'I seek the intoxication one experiences at the parties of the intellectuals and the savants. I don't care a fig for the bloody socialites. On my arrival in Delhi, I remember sipping rum standing next to Swaminathan at Dhoomimal's. Damn it, it was an intoxicating experience! How stylishly he spoke! He was a voluble speaker.'

One day, Dhoomimal threw a party in honour of Mexican poet-thinker Octavio Paz. He hadn't received the Nobel yet, but was quite well-known in Delhi nevertheless. He had also been a diplomat in Delhi and written a poem about a Swaminathan painting.

Paz had grown old, but his wife was young. Pratap and I virtually shadowed Paz at the party. Pratap began to talk about his poetry, and then the mazes, tigers, mirrors, etc., in Borges' work. I soon noticed something unusual. Whenever a photographer approached Paz, he would quickly take off his glasses. Then he whispered his secret to Pratap: 'My wife tells me that I look younger without them.'

Back home at night, for a long time, Pratap was busy relating the substance of his small talk with Paz. 'Baldev, consider this. Such a big poet, a great intellectual and yet he gives so much respect to his wife's unreasonable demands.'

'Why, this is true of all the famous poets, painters and musicians. Once they marry young and attractive women, they face similar worries. They become helpless in front of those beauties. And by the way, even in India the number of such oldies is on the rise. A 70-year-old artist wants to be seen with only a 30-something. While the wife is preparing to leave for a spiritual discourse, he is away having a good time with young beauties in the name of creativity. But surely you are the greatest of them all, Pratap. You are 25, but are ever ready to pour your heart out to anyone between 17 and 70!'

Initially, whenever Pratap approached art galleries, the majority of the managers displayed complete indifference about his prospects on learning about his background.

'Gorakhpur? But where the hell is that?'

'I am sure you know Kushinagar...'

'Kushinagar? Never heard of the place...'

'Then you must have heard about Saraya.'

'Oh my God! Now, what the hell is that? What do these places have to do with modern art?'

'Sir, what can I do about your poor general knowledge? Kushinagar is associated with the life of Lord Buddha. That's where he attained his mahaparinirvana. Saraya commanded an important place in the brief life of Amrita Sher-Gil. And all these places are associated with Gorakhpur. That's where I am from. And mark my words, one day, the collectors from Paris will head to it on a pilgrimage.'

'Young man, I admire your confidence, but you better give up such dreams of grandeur. The real artists come from Baroda, Santiniketan and Bombay, not from Lucknow Art University. If you wish, you can go back to complete a Master's degree there. But you are totally unfit to become a hit in Delhi.'

'I am sure you know about Maqbool Fida Husain. What was the state of the arts in Indore and where is its art school? But when he saw a film on Rembrandt there, he became restive to do something big in the world of art. And on his first visit to Europe, he sobbed like a baby, standing in front of Rembrandt's 11 x 11 feet painting *Night Watch*, hanging in Amsterdam. Today, you would pay the asking price for a Husain, but he is a man with his feet on the ground and so am I.'

Mr Juneja, the owner of the New Star Gallery, took off his glasses and considered Pratap seriously. Then said: 'Buck up, man. Continue your struggle. You too will one day sob like a baby standing in front of a painting.'

'Yes, I shall cry standing in front of Van Gogh's *Sunflowers*.

And you will cry for not having bought one of my paintings on the cheap.'

In 2000, there were early signs of Pratap's success, when he hired two assistants. Even his method of selecting them was quite interesting.

I have been to Europe only twice. Once in 1991, when I had a show in a small town in Britain, and the second time was when I got a residency in France for six months in the year 2000. When I returned to Delhi from France, I discovered that my landlord had put away all my stuff in a store-room and rented out the place to new tenants. 'Shell out the remaining rent and cart away your worthless paintings in a tempo. You always claim that each of your paintings is worth a lakh. I don't think any of them is worth even 500 rupees!'

I approached Pratap and explained my problem. 'Listen, Ballubhai (sometimes he'd address me thus as a tribute to our old friendship), for the time being, I can put you up in my studio. But remember, my two assistants also live there.'

'That's not a problem. I won't say no even if you were to offer to make me an assistant. I'd earn at least 15,000 a month.'

'Sorry, Ballubhai, I can't make you my assistant.'

'And why not? Are you upset with me or what?'

'No, because you are highly gifted. One should never have a talented assistant. I need labourers of art, not artists.' He was quite candid, and right.

I then approached Suhas Hande. He had always expressed gratitude to me for getting him the magical passport to Page Three. 'Come over, yaar, my doors are always open for you.

Stay with me for as long as you wish. You are an intellectual artist. Maybe I'll also learn some of your secrets.'

I immediately loaded my bags and baggage into a tempo and arrived at his studio. Suhas was around 50 and lived alone. His sculptures were not entirely modern in concept, yet in those days, he did manage to obtain some good commissions. Not all Page Three stars sell. Being a Page Three star is an entirely different ball game. One day, *Hindustan Times* carried this caption under a party picture: 'Artist Virendra with a friend.' Actually, Virendra had no value in the art mart, but the person standing with him was Surendra Pal, who had recently received a big prize at the Florence Biennale. So, that's the reality of Page Three.

But Suhas Hande's Page Three avatar turned out to be lucky for him and he always thanked me for it.

I spent a total of four months in his company. He refused to take any rent and food and drinks were on the house as well. But there were occasions when spending an evening with him was nothing less than torture. He had a desperate crush on his 19-year-old maid. And while she would address him as 'Uncle', he fantasized about her. In fact, 'crush' is not the word; he was obsessed with her.

While I stayed with him, he was obsessed with her to the point of being lovesick. In the evening, after a couple of pegs, he would sit on his sofa, crying like a baby. 'Listen, Baldev, I am very serious about her. I want to marry her properly... Want to make her my lawfully-wedded wife. But she doesn't understand my true feelings. She thinks I am old...and makes fun of me.'

'Well, for her you *are* an old man. She calls even me Uncle.'

On my advice, he began to hire the maid(her name was Rashmi)as a model and would pay her well. He made some beautiful sketches of her, but artists being what they are, one day, he couldn't help telling her: 'I want to draw you in the nude. I'll pay double your fee.' I had never given him this advice. That day, Suhas got a 'double' dose of abuse and a tongue-lashing from Rashmi. Looking at her seething with rage, all his romantic fantasies evaporated. That evening, it became all the more difficult for me to put up with his whimpering.

'Look, Suhas, if you want a young model to pose for you in the nude, I can organize one. A journalist friend has the phone numbers of such contacts in his diary.'

'Please, Baldev, try to understand a true artist's feelings. I don't want a streetwalker. I want the innocence, purity, naturalism, and sex appeal, which Rashmi radiates. When she was abusing me this morning, for once I thought she was a stranger and not my Rashmi. My Rashmi is a goddess.'

'To hell with your goddess! You are creating problems for yourself.'

That evening, Suhas revealed another secret. That he had already created a nude sculpture depicting Rashmi. 'The medium is wood. The face is hers. The rest is my imagination. I have kept it wrapped away in a piece of cloth. Haven't shown it to her.'

'Better not show it to her either. That girl won't be able to appreciate the artist in you. You are a Page Three hero and your works have a good market... You better abandon this maid romance or lust.'

'How should I explain it to you, Baldev? This is not lust. It is true that I have drawn amazing sexual pleasure fantasizing about her company at night, but I consider even that as a sign of my pure and divine passion.'

I realized it was difficult to make Suhas mend his ways. Maybe Rashmi needed to wallop him with her slippers to help him leave this 'inspirational' maze.

After about a year and a half, one day, I got a call from a TV reporter. 'Sadanand speaking, crime reporter.'

'Oh ho, people like us follow cultural trends. We have nothing to do with criminals. Has some new fake of Anjolie Ela Menon turned up in the market?'

'No, sir, I want to speak to you about Suhas Hande. I heard that at one time you were staying in his studio. Some people have attacked him in his studio and badly injured him.'

I cut the phone. I was beginning to understand a few things, but didn't want to ask the reporter any questions. Instead, I phoned Pratap Narayan. He laughed wholeheartedly: 'I knew that mediocre sentimental fool would finally end up in this sordid mess. I watched it all on TV and learnt that a mob of Madangir sanitary department staff had barged into his studio, thrashed him mercilessly and destroyed his sculptures. The stupid old man was involved with some young maid.'

I closed the Suhas Hande chapter for good. This time, nothing appeared about him on Page Three, though somewhere in the cluster of Capital News, there was an inch and a half devoted to 'Mob beats up artist'.

I learnt that in the wake of that incident, Suhas quit Delhi. How and in which accident he lost his foot was a matter of numerous speculations. That evening, in the middle of the rain, I watched him as he sat in the cab, forlorn and helpless, his crutches by his side. After handing him 2,000 rupees, I felt I had paid off some debt. I asked him nothing. I was no longer curious about him.

But what to make of this godless world of art? The gallery, which had patronized him, should have at least observed a two-minute silence for him. Instead, wine was flowing, the gallery owner was chirping as usual, and the leading luminaries among the gatecrashers were gorging themselves shamelessly.

Reminiscences of a Gatecrasher

I clearly remember the day—even the date—of the incident. On 26 January 2001, Kutch in Gujarat was shaken by a massive earthquake. Around eight in the morning on that day, I got this call from Pratap Narayan: 'I am sending my car. I think it'll be difficult for you to reach my studio at the Chhatarpur farmhouse on your ramshackle motorcycle.'

'Why so early in the day? What's the occasion? Aren't we evening birds?'

'Baldev, I stopped spending evenings in the old style long ago. I have something important to tell you. I have an exclusive show at Taj Palace Hotel tomorrow evening for just one day. Big-time art collectors among the diplomats have been invited. Also, some guys from Christie's in London. You may not have known much about this. My work has also been selected for the new millennium's first Venice Biennale this year. The show curator is a renowned celebrity in the West. She's also coming.'

Sitting in the car on my way to Chhatarpur, I began to reflect on my lamentable career graph. I had half a mind to tell Pratap that I wouldn't be coming, but thought that I shouldn't appear to be jealous of an old mate's success.

In the days when Pratap was still struggling, a six-foot German diplomat had been floored by my work. She even bought a batch of four paintings at one of my shows at Rabindra Bhavan and paid for them on the spot. She also promised to organize a free official trip to Germany for me. How glorious were those days.

I wasn't a bachelor like Pratap. My wife Shobha was a schoolteacher in Bareilly and my two children stayed with her. She didn't depend on me; rather, I was dependent on her. Her father was one of the leading lawyers in Bareilly. He had always been against our marriage, but when a good-for-nothing artist finally married his talented and beautiful daughter, he didn't want her to move to Delhi to lead a dull life full of deprivations. Yet, for a time, the German diplomat made me such grand promises that I almost called my father-in-law over to Delhi to show him how life was changing for the new-age artists, who no longer had to chop their ears in desperation like Van Gogh, but looked more like prosperous bank managers.

The German diplomat lived alone. One day, she called me to a house party and even gave me a peck on the cheek in the kitchen. That was the high-point of my life as an artist, a magical moment. Thereafter, in my eager enthusiasm, I downed a whole bottle of white wine that evening. I had this misguided belief that white wine didn't give much of a kick. So, I didn't keep count of the number of glasses I had downed.

Next morning, I had to catch the flight to Frankfurt. All arrangements for the 15-day junket had been made by the

German. But I had gotten so sozzled the evening before that even though the alarm clock somehow woke me up, I was in no condition to stand steady. I tried to throw up so my head would lighten. But I just couldn't get up and missed the flight. This was followed by high fever and mumps. I had been to Bareilly a few days earlier and had carried around my nephew, who had been suffering from mumps. Having escaped the infection in my childhood, I had to pay the price now. The doctor tried to scare me: 'You've arrived just in time. You could have ended up becoming impotent.'

'I have two kids already,' I informed him with a smile.

The German diplomat was soon transferred out of India and I began to make advance preparations, so to say, to finally conclude my career as an impotent artist. My downfall had begun. As if that was not enough, in 1999, I fell desperately in love with a married woman. I took it as a heaven-sent opportunity for millennium love and the panacea for my creative impotency. While Pratap prepared to leave for the Venice Biennale, I, a complete asshole, settled down to counting the millennium love's kisses. The consequences were radically tragic. One day, my paramour's journalist husband, an influential man, phoned me: 'I'll send my goons to give you such a thorough treatment that you'll forget all about art. You better stay at least a hundred yards away from my wife.'

Now that I reflect over it, there was another reason for my grand failure—I was trying to follow and fathom the course of the art bazaar on the strength of my superstitious beliefs. Just before one of my major shows at Mumbai's Jehangir Art Gallery, I tried, through a friend's friend, to have an idea of the amount I could expect from the sale of my works. The clairvoyant, claiming to possess Tantric powers, picked up a piece of paper and wrote: '1,07,700.' I was jumping with joy. Finally, though, only two of my paintings found buyers and even these sold on the very last day after I had agreed to heavy discounts.

Then, I fell into the trap of a friend claiming to be a master astrologer. He began to give me all manner of odd suggestions. For example, I must use more blue on my canvases in July; the use of red would bring profits in September and so on.

At one point, deluded by a priest, I took to eating particular kinds of dishes cooked on cow-dung fire and even carried them to feed the deer in the park. Later, I discovered to my horror that the astrologer had made his calculations based on my wrong date of birth.

I wondered who I could blame for my declining career. It soon dawned on me that while I claimed to be a modern artist, in truth, I was quite backward and superstitious. Of course, many of my artist friends also resorted to similar tactics to succeed; I wasn't alone. But by the time I woke up to reality, my art instincts had become blunted and termite had eaten into my creativity. It's an honest confession.

While I had heard reports about Pratap's large studio, it still surprised me when I saw it. Here was a really top-rung artist. How lucky! Pratap had ordered an expensive kurta for me from FabIndia, so I would not look like an indigent gatecrasher at the five-star show.

'Listen, Ballubhai. Don't feel offended. I am not at all trying to humiliate you. You have saved me twice from the jaws of death. This kurta is a small gift on the occasion of my show. And I have also bought a mobile phone for you.'

Unlike now, a mobile phone in those days was not an easily obtainable instrument for housemaids to sit on their haunches and gossip. As a matter of fact, many jokes circulated about mobiles—that Mister So-and-So was spotted making a 16-rupee call to his wife from the vegetable market telling her that since okra was cheaper by five rupees should he buy a kilo of it.

Pratap entrusted me with an additional chore. 'Ballubhai, both of us know every art party gatecrasher in town. They are a pain and spoil the show, as you know. Since I'd be busy with my star guests, you better make sure not a single gatecrasher makes it to my party. You have a free hand. You may even call the security and have the truants arrested if you wish.'

I thought about my new role all night. There was no sleep for me. Pratap and I now lived in two separate worlds. Soon it was three at night, but I was unable to sleep. Ultimately, I had to fall back on the sweet and erotic memories of my millennium love and, as always, resorted to the sleeping pill of masturbation to hit the pillow.

By 2010, I had managed to thoroughly research the Delhi art party gatecrashers, having observed the species from close quarters for some 30 years. When the art market was timid, there were only a handful of them. An old gallery owner would sometimes relate juicy anecdotes about the art parties of the 1970s. The majority of art buyers in those days would be foreign diplomats. The works they bought for 5,000 rupees at the time carried price-tags of lakhs and crores between 2002 and 2007. But that was also the time when only diplomat types would splurge 5,000 rupees to acquire a work of art.

One gallery owner was known to hire call girls for flamboyant diplomats frequenting art parties. He claimed to have observed similar tactics at London and New York book-launch events. The publishers there would hire poison damsels to entice reviewers and the latter were free to take them out to make love and get inspired—with the publisher's compliments.

Of course, the reviewers in India were never in the same league. But an art critic once told me while in his cups that an artist had told him that the receptionist at a particular gallery was on his payroll. 'You are welcome to take her out to have a good time. I'll pay her. You have to only enjoy her services.' The critic was expected to not only write a good or positive review, but also help swing opinion at all committees responsible for handing out prizes, fellowships, scholarships and foreign junkets. That artist also claimed that the art critic of a particular national daily had been gratefully accepting such services for two years.

But the stories of the gatecrashers are even more exciting and no less sordid. And on that historic evening, my task was to ensure that no gatecrasher managed to find his way into Pratap's five-star preview party.

Pratap's party remained the subject of art circle discussions long after it was over. He had now entered another dimension; international collectors had begun to show serious interest in his work.

Once the cycle starts, even the artist gets confused and sometimes, suddenly wakes up in the middle of the night, wondering what was so special about his work that while just a few years ago a collector wouldn't shell out even 5,000 rupees for one of his paintings, today, a crowd of people carrying 50 lakhs queued up outside his door.

One single big-time western collector had changed Pratap's destiny and he was now busy not only painting, but also making videos, sculptures, installations, and creations in many other media.

The gatecrashers at Delhi art parties come in all shapes and sizes. Some are quite high class, arrive in luxury cars, dressed in expensive suits and speak fluent English. But the majority of them have a sort of middle-class background. They have nothing to do with art and only follow the philosophy of eating, drinking and leaving as quickly as possible. Opportunity permitting, they would grab a show catalogue as well. Maybe these catalogues are eventually sold as waste paper. About five or six years after 2002, even minor artists had heavy catalogues issued to push their work and I guess, even their sale as waste paper would have fetched a handsome sum.

These gatecrashers generally try to bring along a companion. This ensures that they do not get bored at the party and the companion is also grateful and thanks the gatecrasher effusively. Over a period of time, these gatecrashers began to form cartels to keep each other informed and updated about forthcoming events. The mobile culture made their task easier. Early birds at a 'wrong' party (one with nothing much to offer by way of food and liquor or where there was strict checking at the gate) would alert their colleagues over the mobile. Quite often, the gatecrashers would tend to fraternize with the caterer to keep track of the parties. The caterer too stood to profit from this arrangement, since thanks to the freeloaders, his bills would be fatter. So for him, it made sense to keep them updated.

One day, I found Mr Narula of Gallerie Forward sitting forlornly, holding his head between his hands. 'Baldevbhai, who are these people who descend in a gang at opening time, don't spend even a single minute in front of any painting, and yet down any number of whisky pegs? Have you noticed how shamelessly the bastards clean out the malaichicken?'

'Narula Saheb, these are Delhi's notorious gatecrashers. You should check them out and then throw them out.'

'Baldevbhai, please try to understand. Ever since that income tax raid on my gallery, I often wonder if they are from that department. Why, on so many occasions, I personally stepped forward to greet them with a smile.'

'You are great, Narula Saheb! Why don't you ask them a few questions? Once you start to do that, these bastards will immediately make themselves scarce.'

Many among them flaunt press cards, whether the paper or magazine they claim to come from exist or not. Others claim to be directors of mysterious companies or call themselves curators. An attractive woman holding a fake bag of a luxury brand would often land up at some galleries. Her visiting card said that she was a curator and the gallery managers would follow her, wagging their tails.

Then there was this large gallery where the gatecrashers gravitated around the door through which food and drinks were brought in. The stuff hardly reached the real guests, since these rogues would conduct their well-organized raids on all the liquor and kebabs before anyone else could lay hands on them.

Poor Preeti Agrawal had managed to rope in the British Council Director to inaugurate her show, and to entertain her foreign guests, had specially organized five bottles of Black Label. Since everybody was busy with the inaugural speeches, when the time came to serve drinks to the guests it was discovered that the gatecrashers had already downed the entire stock and were preparing to flee.

Roopa Bahl of Akashvani was another friend. At one group show (which also had my work), she noticed that I was busy tracking down and catching the gatecrashers. 'Baldevji, this doesn't suit you. You can officially entrust this responsibility to me. I will take care of these bhenchods!' I looked at Roopa in astonishment, then felt reassured. Here was a tough lady.

As the party was ending, Roopa came up to me and handed me 1,500 rupees. 'Baldevji, we earned 3,000. Let's make it fifty-fifty.'

'How come?'

'I called over the centre's security guards and they questioned the freeloaders hogging with abandon. The uninvited ones were forced to pay up. Some did, others ran away.'

I was afraid she might launch forth with some more of her choice expletives, so I quietly pocketed the 1,500. In any case, I had been going round in a cab all day to distribute invitation cards and was happy to recoup at least part of my expenses.

But on that evening at Pratap's party, I encountered an unusual problem tackling a gatecrasher by the name of Sukumar Mathur, who stood there all suited-booted and redolent with perfume. He would often stand next to me at parties, pointing out the professional gatecrashers and explaining how they might have managed to sneak in. He was a gatecrasher himself, but was far smarter than the others of his ilk. For example, he could hold his own in a serious discussion on art.

Sometimes, he imparted quite revealing bits of information to me. For example, I often noticed a black foreigner arrive at evening parties, panting and sweating, lugging along three or four bags. Many a time, he had to leave the bags at the gate. He would arrive, pick up a glass of beer and wolf down malai tikka, all the while keeping a sharp eye on his bags.

Sukumar told me that the bags carried his day's earnings. After collecting gifts and envelopes from numerous parties and press conferences, he would end up in the evening at an art party to refresh himself. So what if he was black, he was a foreigner all the same!

But at Pratap's party, I had to be tough even with Sukumar. 'Do you have an invitation? Pratap has given me strict instructions. So I am helpless today.'

'In that case, congratulations, Baldevbhai. I can't spot a single gatecrasher. This is amazing! You've done a great job!'

I was astonished and no less puzzled. 'Do you have a card? I'm sorry that I have to question you today. But these are orders from the high command.'

Sukumar laughed aloud. 'I am a celebrity gatecrasher. Page Three of the *Times of India* even carried an interview with me.'

'Celebrity gatecrasher? I don't follow you, Mathur Saheb. Which species of art party visitors is this?'

'Do you read the *New York Times*?'

'No, but what has that got to do with the gatecrashers of the Delhi art circuit?'

'Indeed, it has got everything to do with that. That paper once carried interviews with some of the city's professional gatecrashers. And overnight, from gatecrashers, they became celebrities and started receiving proper invitations to parties. But as you know, India is a backward country and therefore, even after becoming a celebrity, I am unable to obtain official invitations. Nonetheless, I am a celebrity and therefore, please don't count me among those two-penny gatecrashers.'

I was left speechless. What convoluted logic! I thought it would be better to give him my own card. It had no name on it. I thrust it into Sukumar's suit pocket. 'Here you are, sir. Here's the first proof of your celebrity status.'

Pratap had been watching our argument for some time. He finally couldn't help it and walked up to me, leaving his guest from Christie's for the moment. 'What happened, Ballubhai? Any problem?' Then he called over a security guard and told him to check Sukumar's card, even as he rushed back to his guest.

Sukumar produced the card from his pocket, picked up a glass of champagne from a waiter's tray and melted into the resplendent crowd. Standing there, the guard watched him for some time. Then turned to me: 'But, sir, the card had no name.'

'Does it matter? What's in a name? He did show you a valid card, didn't he?'

I thought that unusual celebrity at the party would return to me at some point to say 'Thank you'. But perhaps he couldn't break away from the sexy foreigners. He was handsome, dressed smartly and had an Oxford accent. And now he had a card as well.

Lady Six-foot

Pratap's art education took place in Lucknow, whereas I was educated in Benares. I had first noticed him at the Lalit Kala Akademi guest house at Mandi House, where he was busy going through the paces of heavy exercise in the morning. His reasoning: 'If you want a fit brain, you should also keep the body fit. More than the hands, art flows from the mind.'

All his favourite artists were intellectuals—Souza, Swaminathan, K.G. Subramanyan, Gulam Mohammed Sheikh. My belief at the time was that just as an intellectual poet was not really a poet, an intellectual artist was not an artist either. But gradually, in every sphere of art, the influence of the intellectual artist or conceptual art began to dominate. The new age belonged to artists who depended on assistants. The big-time artists operated in a factory, not a studio.

Our landlord lived in the same house as the tiny two-room flat that we had rented in Khirki village. He was a Sikh. He and his wife had the same name—Jaswinder. Jaswinder Singh was a small-time homoeopath. As opposed to her scrawny husband, Jaswinder Kaur tended to continually put on weight. She also continually lamented the absence of a child in their life. She would often make small talk with Pratap. 'When are you going to make my portrait? If you ask me, what's the point of having an artist as a tenant?'

'I'll make one, Bhabhiji, I certainly will. Just give me some time to settle down. A poet has rightly said—*Dil dimaag bhoosa bhar deen, Dilli hamka chaakar kar deen* (My heart and brain are filled with junk, Delhi has turned me into a skunk).' This was Pratap's spin on the lines by Hindi poet, Sarveshwar Dayal Saxena.

There is no denying that he was a voracious reader. He had an enviable collection of serious books, though quite a few of these had been flicked from the library of Prof. Mehta, who taught Art History in Lucknow. When Pratap moved to Khirki, he lovingly wiped his aluminium rack clean and after placing the first book on it—John Berger's *Permanent Red*—bowed to it in the manner of a devotee. Then followed Kafka, Sartre, Camus, and others, and finally it was the turn of Claude Levi-Strauss' *The Savage Mind*, to which he bowed again.

Then he smiled and said: 'Baldev, you have acquired your knowledge of art from Herbert Read, whereas I am a devotee of Marxist art critic and novelist, John Berger.' Well, I certainly had Read's books in my collection, but I had never really even thumbed through them.

Jaswinder Kaur would often pamper Pratap and bring him kheer, gajarhalwa, badamhalwa and other sweet dishes. Occasionally, I would also get to taste a helping or two, but Jaswinder obviously had no faith in me as a painter. When

Pratap showed no inclination to make her portrait for about three months, she couldn't take it any longer. 'What's the use of calling me Bhabhi-Bhabhi all the time? Actually you're good for nothing.'

'Bhabhiji, I will certainly make your portrait. Its market value would be equal to about six months of our rent, but I can offer you a discount. You will have to write off just one month's rent. The portrait will be ready in one day.'

'Devarji, you know very well that Sardarji is a penny-pincher. He won't agree.'

'It's your job to convince him.'

When she broached the subject with her husband, he laced his mild rebuke with a caustic comment: 'You don't understand these modern painters. They don't know how to make a portrait. They draw anything outlandish and claim that it's modern art.'

When Pratap heard it, he picked up his sketch-book, drew a lovely academic-style portrait of Jaswinder Kaur, and handed it to her. From that day on, he was not only served bowls of badam halwa, but aloo parathas as well.

Pratap had a style all his own and I had an entertaining glimpse of it during his 'paid' meeting with Prof. Mehta, who had arrived from Lucknow. I had certainly heard of paid news, but what the hell was this paid meeting?

At our Khirki flat, we received our phone calls on Sardarji's line. If Sardarji was at home, he'd just hang up. When he wasn't around, Jaswinder Kaur would call us over to take it. When Prof. Mehta rang up Pratap one day, he was in the bathroom. As he rushed out, dripping wet with only a towel around his waist, Bhabhiji couldn't take her eyes off his muscular body.

'Sir, this is Delhi, an expensive and ruthless city. It's not Lucknow. Here time is money. I'll spend two hours with you at Volga, you will foot the bill and also pay me 100 rupees as my meeting fee.'

'Come on, is this the way to talk to your professor? And what is a "meeting fee"?' I asked Pratap.

'In Bombay, an art critic starts out by asking for the writing fee. Prof. Mehta is no less of a racketeer. In Lucknow, he would take me out in a rickshaw and regale me with highly intellectual patter. Then one day, thinking that the moment was right, he said to me: "Pratap, in this weather I feel like kissing you." Slimy old bastard!'

'So you allowed him to kiss you?'

'Who do you think I am? An asshole? But the man is well-read. I have learnt a lot from him. Come along if you want. Let's have a good time at Volga. But no beer; the bastard will only offer coffee.'

I laughed: 'Are you sure he won't try to kiss me?'

On the way to Volga, Pratap related numerous anecdotes about Prof. Mehta. I was quite taken by the professor's manner of hiring a rickshaw. Instead of the rickshaw, he would take a close measure of the rickshaw-puller's build and would finally settle for a scrawny one, who wouldn't quibble over the fare. But one day, a bone-bag chose to turn on him with a slipper in hand. Wonder if the professor had demanded a kiss.

Prof. Mehta was not happy on seeing me with Pratap at Volga, but he couldn't do anything about it. Pratap soon got into a serious discussion with him. Finally, when we were about to leave, he told Prof. Mehta without batting an eyelid: 'So, sir, now open your purse and give me my fee.'

Since I was watching, Prof. Mehta became apologetic and said to me: 'I love Pratap's style. When I started working, whenever I would ask my mother for money she'd feel elated. That even though the son was earning, he still begged from her.' Pratap pocketed the 100-rupee note and winked at me.

Many people would see a kind of meanness in Pratap's action, but I certainly enjoyed the paid meeting. That evening, there was chicken curry and a bottle of rum at our studio. And gajarhalwa courtesy Jaswinder Kaur, who was still starry-eyed about Pratap's bare chest.

God knows where Pratap sought out such doddering old men. Around the same time, he stumbled upon an old painter by the name of Siddiqui Saheb at Kwality Restaurant. He was a Sunday painter and since his retirement from government service some 12 years ago, had made it a habit to install himself at Kwality between three and five in the afternoon, when he would have nothing but the choicest Darjeeling tea. Although alone, he would always order two cups; the empty cup would be placed at the other end of the table.

Pratap had to work very hard to unravel the secret of this empty cup. Siddiqui Saheb's inspiration, Salma, had sat there for five years and shared tea with him, until cancer had handed her an untimely death warrant. Siddiqui Saheb now lived on the memories of those days. He would allow Pratap to sit with him, but not on the seat where the empty cup was placed. Pratap had to also put up with Siddiqui Saheb's somewhat odd and silent mode of communing with Salma. All the same, Pratap relished those moments too, though I could never muster enough courage to gatecrash into Siddiqui Saheb's ruminations.

Around the same time, Pratap fell in with another elderly artist. His name was Shyam Lal. He claimed to have seen Amrita Sher-Gil in Lahore 'with my own eyes'. He would be in his studio for a drink every evening and Pratap and I would look for every opportunity to join him. But he was a cussed host and would make a peg with the bottle cap as a measure. Since he had to go to the loo every half an hour, it offered us an opportunity to quickly pour ourselves a Patiala peg. Soon enough, Shyam Lal discovered our ruse and from then on, he would keep the bottle in the kitchen and would only bring out pegs made with the bottle cap.

Shyam Lal hardly spoke about art; most often, he would narrate juicy tales involving the young women he had met during trips abroad in his youth. Pratap would prompt him and eventually, he would enter the realm of graphic detail. And at every meeting, Pratap would also make sure to ask him about Amrita Sher-Gil.

One day Pratap said: 'Sir, Khushwant Singh has written that men are drawn to women of Amrita's fame like iron to a magnet. He says that one day, she landed at his house, went up to the fridge and helped herself to a tankard of beer without so much as a by-your-leave... Is her description as a short and sallow-complexioned woman, with her hair parted in the middle and tightly bound behind, a bulbous nose with visible blackheads, and thick lips with a faint shadow of a moustache correct? She is said to have been attractive, but not beautiful at all.'

'My boys, Shyam Lal was infatuated with Amrita the moment he set eyes on her. If the woman who attracts you is not beautiful, then what is she? Amrita Sher-Gil certainly wasn't Madhubala.'

Pratap was always rewarded with a peg of one and a half caps for bringing up the subject. The condition was that there was to be no argument. And then, Shyam Lal would begin to reminisce about how he kissed his Italian love interest in front of Fontana di Trevi in Rome. And Pratap would use the opportunity to take out more savouries from the fridge.

Around this time, the most interesting event involving Pratap related to Sonali Gupta. Six-foot-tall Sonali was the lover—one might say, the mistress—of a Meerut builder. The builder, Mr Saxena, wanted Sonali to enter the art business. One day, at a party at a farmhouse at Sainik Farms, Pratap noticed Sonali fishing out a half-bottle of Black Label from her handbag to prepare a peg for Saxena. She was herself drinking wine. Saxena didn't want to have the cheap whisky being served at the party. He offered some to Pratap: 'Young man, you may also have the Black Label. You look like a real artist to me.'

That evening, it was decided that Pratap would hold a crash course in art for Sonali in the coming days and would generally teach her the tricks of the trade.

'What about my fee?'

'You tell me, young man… You decide your own fee.'

'Well, I'd like to meet Sonaliji once a week at one of the top—and each time, new—restaurants of Delhi. We'll talk over drinks and dinner. That's all…that's my fee. If you feel like it, you may buy one of my paintings, but that's not a condition.'

'Young man, I hope you won't try to seduce Sonali.'

'No, sir, don't you worry. I don't want to be bashed by a six-foot lady. Moreover, didn't you promise to buy my work?'

Soon enough, Pratap did some research and drew up a list of some leading Delhi restaurants. Then said to me: 'Sorry, Ballubhai…I won't be able to accommodate you in this crash course. Saxena Saheb is quite serious about this. And I might also succeed in offloading some of my paintings.'

Sonali would drive down in her long limo to pick up Pratap. It was quite cumbersome to negotiate the narrow lanes of Khirki in the huge sedan. Jaswinder Kaur was at her wit's end, trying to figure out where the six-foot lady was taking Pratap. I told her that Pratap was her mentor and would teach her the secrets of selling paintings.

'Which means one day Pratap also might own a big car.'

'Why not? You just watch, Bhabhiji…'

In the evening, he had dinner at a posh restaurant and the next morning, Pratap was served badam halwa by Bhabhiji. I thought the time was right to bring up the subject of the first lesson of the crash course. 'Nothing much happened, Ballubhai. We had Chinese and some Scotch. Made some small talk… That's it…'

'Didn't she ask anything about the art market?'

'To hell with the art market! She did bring it up while driving me home: "Pratap, today you didn't mention a word about the art market." But I told her: "Sonaliji, have patience. You'll hear the first word about it after we've been to at least ten restaurants. Why don't you, in the meantime, find your way through the maze of the art bazaar?"'

But Pratap couldn't complete his restaurant circuit. As

luck would have it, the second restaurant on his list was located in Hauz Khas Village. For some reason, Sonali was reluctant to go there. 'I ran a boutique there for two years and am sick of the place.'

Pratap's reasoning was that the restaurant served exceptionally fine Italian cuisine. How could he divine that the taste of the pasta would not last long?

Pratap had barely placed the order and was trying to figure out the range of shades as seen through a glass of red wine, when out of the blue, a four-foot Gujarati woman stormed into the restaurant and headed straight for the six-foot Sonali.

'Do you know me?' she screamed. The waiters and the restaurant manager were horrified.

'Who are you? Why are you screaming? I don't know you.' As she said this, Sonali beckoned the manager. 'Kick this mad woman out. I'm sure she is out of her mind.'

'I'm very much in my senses, madam. So what if you are six feet tall? I can bury you alive right here. I had given you 30,000 rupees worth of stuff for your shop on trust, hadn't I?'

The restaurant's security guard forcibly dragged the woman away. But she would not stop screaming and soon came down to spewing filth. She was hot with rage. Even Pratap suspected that the poor woman might have been wronged and might not be lying.

The dinner held no taste now. Sonali was visibly tense. The security guard told them that while he had thrown her out, the woman had gathered a crowd outside and was sitting in protest, claiming she would not budge until the madam paid up.

Ultimately, Pratap had to summon the police. Once the police van arrived, there was no avoiding going to the Hauz Khas police station, which wasn't very far. One cop took the Gujarati midget away in the van, the other sat with Sonali in the front seat of her luxury car. Sonali took out a 100-rupee note from her purse and tried to force it on the cop. 'Madam, what are you trying to do...'

'Nothing. This is just for some sweets for your kids.'

'But Madam, your complaint has now gone on record and you will have to come to the police station.' He refused to accept the note.

Pratap couldn't figure out what was happening. At the police station, he was in for a bigger shock when the SHO looked at Sonali and the woman and exclaimed: 'So, you've come again! Why don't you arrive at a compromise? Why do you bother us all the time?'

Pratap wondered why Sonali had claimed she didn't know the woman, and even accused her of being out of her mind. He had entered a police station for the first time in his life and left it hurriedly. Half an hour later, Sonali emerged after settling the case and told Pratap: 'I need to go to a good bar.'

The cop on whom Sonali had thrust the 100-rupee note, was now trying to peek into the car through the darkened windows, hoping the madam would re-offer the note. But the madam had changed her mind. Soon, she was screaming at the driver: 'Why don't you move? Bloody bastards! It's the habit of these policewallahs to go on begging!'

Sonali quickly had a couple of vodka pegs in a Defence Colony bar. She was quite tense. While on her way to drop Pratap at his house, she sobbed uncontrollably. 'God knows why this happens only to me. I don't want to open any art gallery. In any case, you aren't giving me any guidance at all, merely hopping restaurants. Even you are cheating me. You are a bloody cheat!' Pratap remained silent. He looked at her diamond ring and realized it was best not to react.

Pratap never saw Sonali after that day. Then one day at a party, he ran into Saxena. He was alone and feigned not recognizing Pratap. Soon, he headed towards a quiet corner, pulled out a hip-flask and took a swig of his expensive brand.

Pratap's first solo exhibition in the capital was dedicated to that Gujarati woman. But the name of Prateeksha Art House, which organized that show, has disappeared from Pratap's records. He erased it himself. Prateeksha's owner, Mrs Sahay, believed in selling a variety of material. Whatever one might say about her, she was the one who had organized Pratap's first show in Delhi. She'd even had a small catalogue and a poster printed for the occasion. The exhibition was called *The Wretched of the Earth*. There was everything at the show—paintings, line drawings, photographs, installations... The only thing missing was Lady Six-foot.

Lady Sweet and Sexy

Mrs Sahay's full name was Asha Sahay. Her husband was a businessman and her only daughter had settled in Sydney after marriage. She wrote poetry as a hobby, had started out as an interior designer, and eventually insinuated her way into the art world. She reminded one of the old-time Hindi film heroines. Indeed, she could often be found sitting in her gallery, raptly listening to old Hindi film songs. With the advent of Facebook, she had even taken to posting old songs on it virtually every day.

She had been in the art business for quite a while, but the leading Delhi galleries looked down upon Prateeksha Art House. Interestingly, the first (even if a rather small) exhibition of India's now internationally-acclaimed and leading artist, Pratap Narayan, was organized by none other than Asha Sahay. But a couple of years later, Pratap removed her gallery's name from his bio-data. On the occasion of his first exhibition, Asha had made numerous phone calls to somehow make sure at least one painting of the dashing young artist sold. Those were the days when even 3,000 rupees would revive an artist's flagging fortunes. Finally, she did manage to sell a canvas for 5,000 and was on cloud nine that day and offered samosas to all her staff. Her specialty was daal samosas; Dhoomimal Gallery was known to serve the aloo ones.

Asha Sahay had sold some of my works as well and generally made good money in the days of the art boom. I remember she bought a work by Jogen Chowdhury for three lakhs and within days, sold it for 23. Nevertheless, in the eighties, art still moved at a snail's pace. It was counted as a great event if one could afford to throw a party on the show's opening day.

Asha had told Pratap: 'The very name of your show is depressing—*The Wretched of the Earth*. You should have chosen some sweet name and come up with some nice, matching paintings.'

'We have named you Lady Sweet and that much sweetness is enough for the purpose of art, I guess. Life's reality is quite bitter, Ashaji, but if you want, you may continue to wallow in the sweet treacle of life. It'll make no difference.'

Asha Sahay was more of a housewife. She'd often declare that once she retired, she would publish a novel offering a grand exposé of all the art world's secrets. 'If I publish it today, it'll be a nightmare for me to survive,' she would say.

She would also impress upon everyone in the course of a conversation that she shared all the day's small talk and incidents with her husband. 'I report to him on everything and every subject during our morning walk. He rather enjoys all the colourful anecdotes of our world.'

Our dear Pratap Narayan had all manner of tricks up his

sleeve to leave an opponent speechless. He said: 'You're a triple-S, Ashaji…'

'What do you mean? What's this triple-S?'

'Sweet, sensuous and sexy.'

'Pratap, you're a loud mouth! You say anything you like… For heaven's sake, look at my age.'

'I'm telling you the truth, Ashaji. You don't need to be shocked. Even at this age, when you bend down to pick up anything, you reveal a marvellous cleavage.'

Asha Sahay fell silent. But Pratap was tickled and wondered whether she would relate this conversation to her husband uncensored or would suitably alter it. Her husband was a happy-go-lucky guy with a great sense of humour. He may not have bothered or gotten upset on being told what Pratap had said.

Those were the days when every young artist, who landed in Delhi from Bengal, Bihar or Orissa with bundles of his works, ultimately knocked on Asha Sahay's door. She'd pay them very little, but enough for a needy artist to survive. There were expenses like buying a return ticket to one's hometown or hiring a taxi or an auto to hop galleries. Asha Sahay would give some advance to the cash-strapped artist to lighten his burden and would top that up with a liberal supply of daal samosas. Her advice to young artists: 'If you approach a gallery looking like a needy artist, no one's going to look at you. Approach them with confidence, as if you need absolutely nothing. Once the gallery owner figures out that you're needy, you're done…'

Pratap told Asha about a notorious art collector, who on the last day of a show, would land up at Jehangir Art Gallery in Mumbai with a pick-up truck. He knew where the artist from Indore or Pilibhit would take his load of 40 paintings. This was the time to strike a good bargain and, most often, he succeeded.

Asha Sahay's gallery also sold the works of leading artists picked up from the secondary market. But she specialized in promoting young artists. In the golden days of the art boom, she would claim to have exposed the true face of top-rung galleries. 'They too hawk B-grade artists, but quietly, without making a noise about it. The reality behind the façade is quite different... After all, I was the one who had organized Pratap Narayan's first solo show in Delhi. He may have forgotten it, but the history of art cannot be tampered with. I've made history. It's another matter that if I were to phone Pratap Narayan today, he won't take the call.'

One morning in 2007, Asha Sahay sent her car to fetch me for lunch. Around the time she had organized Pratap's exhibition, he had made three sketches in her sketchbook, but hadn't signed them. In fact, two of them were drawn in front of me. Nobody could question their authenticity. Asha said to me: 'I have been trying desperately to contact Pratap, but it has become impossible to get through to him. A collector is interested in buying them, but as you know, they are unsigned. I need a certificate of authenticity; he is offering a very good price.'

Asha now took out a wad of 50,000 rupees from her table drawer. 'The collector is willing to buy the drawings if you authenticate them. I'll pay your fee right here. I want to close this deal. Today, everyone is making money in Pratap's name. At least I can honestly claim to have held his first show in Delhi and therefore can also claim some privileges.'

What I had to authenticate was not something fake. Moreover, 50,000 rupees meant a lot to me at the time. I had to pay off a hefty loan. If everybody was making money, why not me? After all, the art buyers were no Mr Squeaky Cleans either.

I immediately authenticated the drawings. I hadn't done anything unethical. Asha said: 'Baldevji, I was prepared to pay some cash to Pratap himself. But his PA never came back to me.'

At this point, I imposed a small condition on the collector—he should refrain from selling the drawings for at least three years. He assured me: 'Don't worry, Baldev Sir. They won't appear in the market for ten years. You can trust me.'

The collector had also brought along his girlfriend. The deal went through smoothly. I told Asha: 'Today, I won't settle for samosas. Take me to some high-class restaurant.' We really celebrated the amazing deal.

Three months later, as I was sitting with an old artist friend in Udaipur, I got this call from Pratap: 'Where are you, Ballubhai? Aren't you in Delhi?'

'No, I'm in Udaipur. Tell me, anything important?'

'Yes, there is. I have been contacted by a Mumbai art dealer. Asha Sahay sold three of my drawings from her collection at a fancy price. I have also been told that you authenticated them. You should have at least checked with me. I would have paid you more than Asha—these days you also get paid for declining to authenticate.'

'But do you ever pick up your phone? Even your PA never reverted to Asha Sahay. What could we do?'

'Look, now those drawings are coming up at an auction. I had never gifted them to Asha. Nor did she buy them. Then how could she sell them? This is not on. It's a fraud. And I'm sorry to say you are also part of this fraud.'

'Pratap, I am not part of any fraud. Those drawings were made by you and I merely issued a certificate of authenticity. If you did not give them away as a gift or did not sell them, you are free to drag Asha to court. If you want, you may include my name as well. I'm prepared to face the consequences. I am sick of these art market tricks. By the way, Asha tried her best to get in touch with you. Why don't you file an FIR? Let us find out our worth. At best, we might go to jail. Would you have been happy if Asha had thrown the drawings away in the dustbin or set them on fire or destroyed them?'

I cut the phone. Then I contacted Asha. The collector blamed his girlfriend for being in too much of a hurry to get rid of them. But, as the saying goes, the arrow had left the quiver.

Subsequently, two of the three drawings sold at a very high price at the auction. Pratap and the auctioneer had come to an arrangement. Pratap was mollified as one of the drawings was returned to him. These were rare drawings of his early period. Now, a massive volume on his oeuvre was coming out in Germany and it included all three of them— properly signed by Pratap. That's how this episode ended.

After this incident, Asha Sahay's sympathy for me increased. While she was not inclined to buy my paintings ('What to do! The market winds are quite contrary, though if you ask me, I like everything'), she had some rare works in her collection and told me: 'If you help me in offloading them, you may earn a hefty commission. All artists are into this side business. Why are you determined to remain a struggler?'

I remember many interesting and memorable incidents of this period. I was even witness to the ruthless face of the art world and once saw it from close quarters.

Among Asha Sahay's contacts was a big-time elderly collector. Asthana Saheb was known for landing up at an artist's place and buying up all his works before loading them in a truck. He had a good nose for art and paid in cash. His one particular remark had become a jocular quote in the art market: 'I had him cleaned out,' meaning, he had bought all of an artist's work. His driver would sit outside in his car with cash in hand. The moment Asthana Saheb phoned him, he'd walk in with the cash and arrange for a truck. Many a time, he'd carry sacks full of wads of 10-rupee notes. Once the art bazaar began to rise, Asthana switched to bags bulging with 500-rupee notes.

One day, Asthana phoned me out of the blue. 'Baldevji, I'd be at your studio today at 11 in the morning. Please keep yourself free.'

I smiled. 'Asthana Saheb, are you meaning to clean out my studio?'

'That's also possible. If you'd give me a chance.'

I quickly pulled out all my old works. I was sick of carrying the burden of my art. I often dreamt of that Japanese art collector, who overnight changed the life of an artist by buying up all his works at enormous prices.

Asthana was quite a stickler for punctuality. He would

walk slowly, because of a limp and had some trouble coming up the stairs, but somehow made it to my third-floor flat, though by then he was out of breath. 'It is quite an exercise to reach some artists' studios. But it's good for me.'

Asthana spent some two and a half hours going through my works. He considered everything—paintings, watercolours, sketchbooks. Even some photographs taken by me. I had often noticed Asthana at art shows but had never spoken to him.

I was totally deluded into believing the little voice in my head telling me: 'Baldev, your days of struggle are over. Everything will go today. Soon, the driver will be here with a sack full of notes, then a truck will arrive and I'll be off exploring new avenues of art. I won't mind even 10-rupee wads, provided the godforsaken sack is brought up!' I needed someone who would clean me out. And clean me out completely. Both my brains and my studio. It was difficult to carry such a heavy burden of art.

But the crafty Asthana had other ideas. After seeing all my works, he said: 'Baldev Saheb, you seem to be hiding your real treasure. Why don't you bring that out as well? This is the right time. We could cut a deal right now.'

'Asthana Saheb, I don't follow you. All my work is in front of you. I have no wish to hide any of it. You are the first collector to scrutinize my work so closely...'

'What I mean is, this is the time to bring out the treasure trove of Pratap Narayan's works you've been hiding all these years and we have a deal. You'll be a rich man. Asha told me you might have some old works by Pratap Narayan, but don't normally show that treasure to anyone.'

I cannot describe my disappointment at that moment. I had no works by Pratap. It took me half an hour to convince Asthana that I was not lying. He finally stood up after my confession.

'So, you have absolutely no interest in my work?' I asked him, begging abjectly.

'I can pay four lakhs, but you have to decide right now.'

'Which particular painting are you interested in?' I was really naive.

Asthana had valued 124 of my works collectively at four lakhs. The same man was ready to shell out 15 lakhs for just one of Pratap's paintings.

'Asthana Saheb, your offer doesn't even cover the cost of my material. This is highly unjust.'

'I am not compelling you, Baldevji. The point is, we don't fix the price. The market forces fix them. Your luck also might turn one day. Until then, carry on with your struggle and learn from Pratap.'

After Asthana left, I felt like bawling. His visit had left me shell-shocked. Asha Sahay was repeatedly calling me on my mobile, but I was in no mood to speak to her. I phoned my wife: 'I am quitting Delhi to come back to Bareilly. Enough of this art-shart...'

'And what are you going to do here?'

'Tell me, if I open a stall of Amritsari kulche-chhole in Bareilly, how much do you reckon I might make?'

'No chance. Those who wanted to open such stalls already have. You carry on in your world of art. Even the children are happy here, telling everyone that their dad is a painter like Husain Saheb. They certainly don't need a poor kulche-chhole-hawking dad.'

It was a really dark evening for me and I felt drained. For the first time in my life, I thought I should set fire to all my works one by one. At night, Asha Sahay called up again and revived some sweet hopes. She claimed to have got hold of five works by a much-sought-after South Indian artist. 'If you try, both of us can reap a bonanza.' She asked me to have a meeting with art collector Raghavji. He was recuperating in a hospital and his condition immediately improved, once he heard Krishna Iyer's name. He told me: 'I am sending my car right away. Come over to the hospital with all his works. You rarely find his works in the market, though I already have 15.'

Raghavji is quite well known in Delhi as an avid collector. Many people claim that he helped Lakshmi Mittal acquire some prized works of Indian art in London. He was not in the hospital for any serious condition, but merely for a general check-up and to recoup his health.

In December 1988, Husain Saheb had had his open-heart surgery done in the newly-opened Escorts Hospital. On New Year's Day in 1989, Pratap and I visited him. We had a fine catalogue of our group show printed and wanted Husain Saheb to release it. He agreed to do so from his hospital bed. I had met Raghavji for the first time there, in Husain Saheb's hospital room.

That very evening, Safdar Hashmi was attacked and murdered. At that time, Pratap made a painting dedicated to Hashmi, though thereafter, his political inclinations gradually ran to seed. He had come to realize that in the art world, it was more important to be practical than to advertise one's political leanings.

Raghavji came up with a very low offer for Krishna Iyer's works. 'I could pay five lakhs. If anyone offers more, please let me know, though I am sure no one will offer more.'

A big Mumbai gallery eventually bought the works for eight lakhs. I didn't inform Raghavji. Asha Sahay settled my dues straight away.

Six months later, the same works by Iyer sold at very good prices at an auction at a five-star hotel in Delhi. Raghavji was there at the party. He came up to me, held my hand and said: 'Just because you didn't sell the works to me doesn't mean I couldn't have them. Did you notice, I have bought the finest painting in the lot at the auction?'

'Yes, Raghavji, I did notice and I quite follow the politics of these auctions. Today you have acquired one work for eight lakhs. That day, you had offered me only five lakhs for all five. Do you think I don't understand the arithmetic? You have quite a few of Iyer's paintings and have simply raised their market price.'

Raghavji merely smiled and moved over to Asha Sahay and began to discuss the morning walk with Lady Sweet and Sexy.

The Cake of a Fake and the Green Parrot

When the art market flourishes, so does the business of fakes. This is the universal truth. Once artists discover that they are in increasing demand, they start hiring assistants, who in turn, opportunity permitting, become active in the business of churning out fakes. But they have their sob stories too. Their primary complaint is that while their boss has fun with socialites and fattens his bank balance selling his works at fancy prices, they are the ones actually sweating it out in the studios on low wages. All the same, the assistants counted for nothing on their own.

Pratap was well-versed in the ways of the West and did not mind his assistants continuing to paint on his canvases even when there were visitors around. They were free to notice them. His basic theory was that in modern art, it was the concept or the idea that counted and technical virtuosity was secondary.

But quite a few eminent artists do not disclose they have

an assistant. At one camp, I had met a talented young artist called Naresh Mishra. A few days later, he ran into me again in a posh South Delhi colony. I was middle-aged by now, so he bent down to touch my feet.

'What are you doing here, Naresh?'

'Sir, I've got a job.'

'With whom? The four big artists in this colony certainly don't have any assistant.'

'Sir, please don't tell anyone. I am helping Mahesh Srivastava in his studio on 20,000 a month.'

'That's very good. Why are you so secretive about it, though? Pratap quite openly gets his works done by assistants.'

'You are right, sir, but Maheshji has told me strictly to not disclose this to anyone.'

One day, I arrived at Mahesh's studio unannounced and found Naresh working there. Even as he greeted me—I had told him never again to touch my feet—Mahesh said: 'A talented boy. Comes over on weekends to take some lessons. I like to promote young artists.'

In those days, one high-profile artist (i.e. hit at auctions, where his works sold like hot cakes) would never allow anyone even to enter his studio. Once, when I was supposed to meet him at his studio in relation to his own work, he asked me a dozen questions and finally imposed the condition that I must arrive alone. 'Many bastards steal your ideas.'

One of Pratap's assistants was from my town. In fact, it was I who had recommended Suresh Babu to Pratap. One morning, I learnt that with the art market heading skywards, Suresh Babu had suddenly decided to quit Pratap's well-paying job. I called Suresh over to my house. What was the catch?

Pratap had once introduced me to a beautiful fashion designer at Rabindra Bhavan. He told me: 'Suneeraji is a good lady. Do help her if you can. She wants to open a very large gallery.' But the first person she stabbed in the back on opening the gallery was none other than Pratap. She signed a contract with his assistant, Suresh Babu, on a salary of 50,000 rupees a month. Pratap was paying him merely 15,000. Suneera was planning to inaugurate her gallery with the works of Suresh Babu. The media had been bought over with reports that Suresh Babu was the next Pratap Narayan of the Indian art scene. On the inaugural day, Suresh Babu was all smiles, standing next to Suneera, flaunting a suit stitched in Bangkok.

'Glad to see you have arrived,' I told Suresh Babu. He seemed to feel guilty and said: 'Sir, I don't know why luck hasn't favoured you in the art market, but my heart says that one day your works will also command high prices.'

I was crest-fallen when, soon after, Suresh Babu cajoled me into selling him an old painting of mine against cash payment. 'I also want to start a personal collection like Pratap's.'

One evening, Suresh Babu was at my studio in an expansive mood; after a few pegs, he lost his way and opened up, telling me numerous stories involving Pratap. These were all new; I knew the old ones by heart. He also told me that he had made a painting for Pratap, but had given it to Suneera instead, who had sold it at an auction in London for a huge sum. While it is true that the concept and style of Pratap's works had become brands across the world, the reality was that it was Suresh Babu who had been churning out Pratap's paintings for quite some time. Pratap merely approved and signed them. Technically, the painting Suneera had sold at the London auction was a fake only in the sense that Pratap had not approved and signed it, while his 'approved' paintings currently in the market had all been painted by Suresh Babu. Which meant that there was only a hairline difference between the fake and the real.

Pratap had once explained to me psychiatrist David Cooper's interesting theory about the difference between an insane being and a genius. Within a circle, towards the bottom, right in the middle there was a point where insanity and genius stood very close to each other. Why, they nearly touched each other; one might even say, were almost identical. But there was a world of difference between the intellectual level of the two. The genius had arrived at that point after completing its journey. It had traversed the entire circle and overcome all the hurdles. But the person who was insane had got 'arrested' half way through and had virtually fallen to that point. He was very close to being a genius and yet, in reality, far from it.

It thrilled me, as I rationalized that the Cooper theory Pratap had advanced was the very theory, which could explain the difference between the fake (insane) and the real (genius). But who was responsible for the 'arrest' of the fake? The artist himself 'arrested' it and dragged it to the point near the original work, albeit in a confused state. If society is responsible for the insane, the artist has to take responsibility for the fake.

After the fourth peg, Suresh Babu was very much in form. He drew closer to me and said: 'There's no denying Pratap

Bhaiyya paints very well, but how would he find time to paint nowadays, busy as he is chasing women and awards and going off on foreign jaunts? His works now sell solely on the strength of his name, no matter who actually paints them. Only last year, he made that famous series titled *The Girl and her Green Parrot*. Actually, I am the one who painted the entire series. I am responsible for each painting. Pratap didn't even touch them. Today, you can't lay hands on the complete series of 36 together in the market. But if I want, I can offload another set and there'd be a flutter.'

'But Suresh Babu, the concept is not yours...'

Suresh Babu convulsed with laughter and told an interesting story. It was all about a girl called Kamla, whose mother was a maid in Pratap's studio. Pratap would often help her. Once, when she fell sick, she began to send her nineteen-year-old daughter in her place. Kamla was beautiful, intelligent and sensitive. But Pratap, as always, was so busy that he never bothered to even look at her. In the meantime, an Italian woman called Lalla, who was working on an encyclopaedia of contemporary Indian art, got involved with Pratap or one might put it this way—Pratap got involved with her. She lived in Pratap's studio and would communicate with Kamla in sign language. On a couple of occasions, in the course of her dialogue with Pratap, she also brought up the subject of Kamla's acute intelligence and stunning beauty.

One day, Lalla learnt from Kamla that she had a pet at home—a lovely green parrot in a cage. On a spur, Lalla decided to visit Kamla at her house and spent hours capturing the parrot's images in her camera—solo and in the company of a smiling and resplendent Kamla. Then she made large archival prints of the same and showed them to Pratap. 'I am planning to exhibit them in Rome.'

Pratap closely examined those photographs for about an hour. Finally, he told Lalla: 'No, let me work on a series of paintings showing the girl and the green parrot. These will be 36 miniature-sized works. I'll also make use of your photographs and give you credit, apart from paying you for the photographs, of course.'

Lalla was more interested in the credit. A huge show of Pratap's works was planned in Florence. She agreed to Pratap's proposal. Pratap again closely looked at the photographs, then said: 'You see, Lalla, this'll be a very erotic series that will put *Kama Sutra* in the shade.'

'No, Pratap, you can't do that. This girl regards me very highly and trusts me implicitly. She also has a lot of respect for you.'

'Lalla, I am not going to ask her to model for me. This is India. There would be a riot if I did that. A film star had to go to jail because of his maid. No, I have no such designs.'

Pratap now called over Suresh Babu to explain his concept. Some paintings were to be largely straight copies of the photographs, except that the colour scheme was to be organized in a particular fashion. In some of the imaginary paintings, the green parrot was to be imposed in a certain way on the girl's breasts, thighs, private parts, hips, etc. 'Suresh Babu, I'm not looking for pornography. Some of the images in the series will be just barely erotic. They ought to convey both poetry and a certain element of eroticism. You need to show that the parrot has entered every part of the girl's body...' Then turning to Lalla, he said: 'Wonderful idea, Lalla, you're great!'

The following day, Pratap and Lalla left for Cambodia and Suresh Babu set about working on the series with no thought for anything else. Indeed, he completely immersed himself in the series, so Sir would be overjoyed on his return and he would be justified in asking for a big reward.

For the first five days, Suresh Babu consciously tried to hide the set of photographs taken by Lalla. He was afraid Kamla might create an issue, without realizing he was in for a bigger reward. When the gods are kind, they don't just shower blessings, they send them in a cloudburst.

Suresh Babu was a bachelor and a virgin to boot. Whenever he was seized with an irrepressible urge, he would either begin to recite the Hanuman Chaalisa or would thrust his head under a cold-water tap. He had a muscular body and was determined to use all his energy to complete Pratap's series.

One day, Kamla went on leave. The occasion was Bhaiyya Dooj. Suresh Babu was happily working on the series. Lalla's photographs were lying around on the floor and complete as well as incomplete canvases were stacked around haphazardly. Amir Khan Saheb's *Raag Hansdhvani* was playing on the music system.

No, let no one be under any illusion. Suresh Babu was a Bareilly yokel, whose own choice would have been '*Jhumka gira ra Bareilly ke bazaar mein*'. Why, initially, he listened only to such songs on his cassette player—'*Jumma chumma de de*', '*Roop tera mastana*' and so on.

Then one day, Pratap gave him a scolding. 'Suresh Babu,

this won't do. When in my studio, you will only play Amir Khan, Bhimsen Joshi, Kumar Gandharva and the like. Have you ever listened to Mozart's 40th symphony, Suresh Babu? You'd start shitting bricks.'

From that day on, Suresh Babu began to savour classical music on Pratap's imported music system. And soon enough, he took to crooning Amir Khan's *Raag Hamsadhvani* even in the bathroom!

On Bhaiyya Dooj, while Suresh Babu swam in the ocean of high-class romantic melodies, guess who walked into the studio in a theatrical manner? Our low-class Kamla. But Suresh Babu was unaware that in the course of sweeping the studio, Kamla too had become a minor member of that high-class club.

Unbeknownst to Suresh Babu, Kamla silently watched the proceedings for about 15 minutes. The painting Suresh Babu was busy with was entirely erotic. It had the green parrot sitting on Kamla's left thigh. All of a sudden, Suresh Babu noticed Kamla and was totally flustered. *She'll definitely thrash me with her slippers today*, he thought.

'*Arre*… You didn't visit your brother on Bhaiyya Dooj?'

'Good that I didn't…'

Suresh Babu was so confused that he thought of asking Kamla to put the vermilion mark of Bhaiyya Dooj on his forehead instead. In any case, he didn't have a sister. 'Tell me, Kamla, why is that good?'

'If I hadn't come today, I wouldn't have seen this painting. I was already suspecting you were hiding something from me.'

'No, no… Nothing of the sort, Kamla. Why should I hide

anything from you? Actually, this is Pratap Sir's idea. You know very well that I do whatever the boss wants me to do. It was his order... Try to understand, Kamla. This is the truth of life.'

Suresh Babu was ready for a 'slippery' thrashing. He had even factored in the fact that a painting or two might get damaged in the process and was mentally prepared to paint them again. Next time, he'd keep his trunk under lock and key, if only the gods would save him this once!

But Kamla's response was quite unexpected: 'Sir, if you want, shall I fetch the parrot from home? You'd enjoy painting this better and the parrot would enjoy it too.'

Suresh Babu peered at Kamla closely. *What am I scared about?* He took no time in handing Kamla a 500-rupee note. 'Hire a taxi or an auto and bring the parrot quickly. And yes, you like pizzas, so bring one along.'

'Shall I also bring along a couple of my dresses Mitthu fancies?'

'Yes, yes. Bring them too. Quick.'

'But sir, you haven't put any dress on the girl...'

'Try to understand. She is not shown naked in every painting, only in a handful. In the others, she is dressed. Bring them. They might come handy if Mitthu were to like them and I'll also get the real inspiration. I have been wasting time like an idiot copying these photographs.'

Kamla rushed out with the 500-rupee note in hand and breezed in breathless. She carried everything—the dresses, the pizza, the parrot and the cage.

'I've heard artists pay their models handsomely.'

Suresh Babu had now entered another universe. Pratap

often told Suresh Babu that he always had a very odd smell about him. He had therefore purchased an expensive perfume; he was redolent with its scent by the time Kamla was back, carrying the parrot. He considered Kamla's statuesque body and told her in English: 'Yes, you look like a beautiful model to me.'

Suresh Babu figured that he should first make friends with Mitthu the parrot. The girl would automatically follow into the trap. So he devoted the next two days to patiently pampering Mitthu.

'You seem to like Mitthu more than you like me. You're very naughty, sir.'

Kamla's vocabulary included English words like 'ouch', 'shit', 'fuck', 'naughty' and many more. Suresh Babu finally mustered enough courage to blurt out: 'Kamla, my darling, you are very, very sexy.'

I thought Suresh Babu was overly spicing the tale. The fifth peg had taken him to seventh heaven. 'You see, Baldev Sir, this is all I can call my achievement after sweating it out in Pratap Sir's studio. I didn't make much money there, but Kamla certainly gave me a glimpse of real heaven.'

After a while, Suresh Babu stated that Kamla had since married, was happy and was a big fan of *Bigg Boss* on TV. 'She even asked me once how come I hadn't yet managed to get onto *Bigg Boss*.'

After his 'glimpse of heaven', Suresh Babu put all his efforts into the series. He would time and again tell Pratap to enjoy himself among Cambodia's temples. 'I want to give you a surprise on your return.'

Pratap had gone there initially for only four days, but it

took him three weeks to return. He was amazed when he saw the series. But while the catalogue eventually had the names of both Lalla and Kamla, there was no mention of Suresh Babu.

'Sir, this series should have my name too. I have worked very hard on it.'

'I've brought a bottle of single-malt whisky for you. It's quite expensive. Also a box of wine chocolates. Have fun. What's there in a name?'

Suresh Babu was deeply hurt. Even as he told me all this, he began to cry. I somehow pacified him and he said: 'Sir, every day, I would personally give bites of wine chocolates to Kamla. It was a large box and I somehow believed it would never get exhausted... The moment she sucked the chocolate, her eyes would light up with an uncanny, intoxicated look.'

I thought Pratap had deprived himself of a big pleasure. He was after Lalla without realizing how much pleasure the girl with the green parrot was giving to his assistant, that pumpkin-like retard No. 1! I knew it, because I too had wasted any number of liquor chocolate boxes in my great Millennium Love phase.

But this story ended on a tragic note. One day, Suresh Babu found himself behind bars. Pratap had levelled quite serious charges against him. He was arrested for painting fakes. It was the first time an eminent artist had had his assistant sent to jail.

I phoned Pratap and, surprisingly, he picked up my call. 'Yes, Ballubhai, I knew you'd phone. But I couldn't have remained silent. I was under pressure from a London gallery.' Gradually, as we spoke, we found ourselves switching from informal expressions to formal terms of respect. Our distance was increasing.

'But why didn't you have Suneera arrested? Is it because she is moneyed and powerful? She is the real culprit. She is the one who used Suresh Babu. You know very well that you paid Suresh Babu a pittance for his efforts. You exploited him. And now you've had the poor man sent to jail. He'll go out of his mind.'

'It isn't easy for me to have Suneera arrested. Of course, she has cheated me and I'll fix her in my own time. But Suresh Babu is going to face a new charge. Kamla is now going to depose against him. I won't spare him. I want the world to know the taste of the cake of fake art.'

Predictably, Suresh Babu went out of his mind. Somehow, he managed to be released from jail after six months; Kamla had refused to bring the charge of sexual exploitation against him. But he was no longer fit to paint. He went back to Bareilly. People say he has become insane. He would sometimes write 'I am the real Pratap' in big bold letters on the back of his kurta and roam about in a deranged manner. He had also discovered some 'healthy' tricks of getting hold of free liquor. When a liquor shop was about to close for the day, he'd park himself outside with an already-purchased bottle, and sell it to one of the customers at a premium, earning his own quota free.

Therefore, I still feel he has not gone completely insane. At least some traces of intelligence remain. One day, when he came down to Delhi to meet Suneera, her guards began to bash him up. While he was being kicked about, Suneera was seen quickly getting away in her huge limo.

Love Letter to a Father

Anyone can write a love letter to his sweetheart. Some consult manuals for the purpose, some cajole their friends to write one for them, some pen them in the routine filmy style and some are entirely driven by emotional nonsense when their hare-brained impulses are at their peak. But have you ever heard of a man writing a love letter addressed to his sweetheart's dad? The young and naïve Pratap was one such person, who made this historic move. In his early days, well-known artist Brajesh Bhai had allowed Pratap working space in his large studio. He was a name to reckon with in Delhi's art circles, though Pratap only gave him four and a half marks out of ten as a painter.

'And what's this four and a half business?'

'Haven't you watched Fellini's *Eight and a Half*? My four and a half are somewhat in the same vein.'

'You have forcibly occupied his studio.'

'Baldev, you'll never fully understand me. I always think of the future.'

When Pratap and I shared a flat, I witnessed my first

miracle, when one fine morning, Brajesh Bhai, a portraitist par excellence, appeared unannounced in front of our building in his old Ambassador and began to honk. I shouted from the balcony: 'Sir, Pratap is in the bathroom.'

'But I had told him to be ready by eight.' He came up and began to closely look at our few possessions. I ran out to prepare tea. Brajesh Bhai had a vast network of contacts and the art world sprang to action on one signal from him.

A journalist friend of ours, Jasdev Singh, had recently returned from America and had gifted me an issue of *Playboy* with the remark, 'Since my daughter has now grown up, my wife doesn't want such dangerous material lying around the house, and it's difficult to hide it. But nudes can be useful to artists like you. They might even inspire you.' That morning, as Brajesh Bhai sat there, an issue of the London art magazine *Studio* was on the table, and next to it gleamed the latest issue of *Playboy*.

When I returned from the kitchen carrying tea, I found Brajesh Bhai busy savouring *Playboy's* contents. I felt uneasy and placed the cup on the table rather nervously. But Brajesh Bhai betrayed no nervousness. 'For Indians like us, only two things represent freedom on landing in a foreign country— Scotch whisky and *Playboy*. On my trip to London last year, I ran into Reddy the painter at the British Council offices. He invited me over to his hotel, but I arrived there half an hour early. The poor guy was unprepared to receive me at that moment. And guess what I found on his table—a bottle of Scotch and the latest issue of *Playboy*. He wanted to hide them, but I interrupted him: "Even I do the same as soon as I land in London—organize a Scotch and a *Playboy*."'

I felt reassured. Brajesh Bhai appeared to be quite forward-thinking. I had been worrying for no reason. As he turned the pages, he stopped at a full-page nude. 'Baldev, to tell you the truth, I enjoy them immensely.'

'What is it, sir? What do you enjoy immensely?' Suddenly I was filled with a sense of freedom. 'I would also like to see.'

'Are you sure you won't laugh?'

'No, sir, I have a very high regard for you. Your portrait of Sardar Patel the Iron Man is a wonderful work.'

'That's precisely why I am afraid you might start laughing when I tell you what I like.'

'No, sir, I don't believe you. Your liking can prove to be a big inspiration for us.'

'Listen, then, I am fascinated by these women's pubic hair. I quite enjoy looking at it. When I visited Japan and bought a *Playboy*, I discovered they had censored the pubic hair in each photograph and put their stamp exactly there. And this, in a country, which considers even pornography a form of art. When I tell this to Pooja's mom, she comes after me with a broom. No one understands an artist's tragedy.'

'You are right, sir.'

'So you also like it?'

What could I say? I almost whispered to him: 'Sir, every artist likes it. It's something natural. I have seen French and German films where even top heroines strike such poses.'

'Is that so? Where do you get to watch them?'

'At Max Mueller Bhavan and Alliance Française. All leading filmmakers show such things.'

'Next time, take me along. I've hardly ever watched art films.'

This dialogue could have turned complicated, but just then, Pratap showed up. That morning, Brajesh Bhai had come to give Pratap his first driving lesson.

On his return home, I began to pull his leg. 'Your father-in-law-to-be is an admirer of pubic hair.'

'Shut up!'

'Oh my God! He was quite open about his preference. I'm not joking.'

At that time, Pratap claimed to be friends with Brajesh Bhai's only daughter, Pooja. She was a graphic artist. When Brajesh Bhai proposed to give Pratap driving lessons, it set me thinking. Why would such a prominent artist arrive early in the morning to offer lessons to a young and upcoming artist? To tease Pratap, I told him: 'Why should he disclose his preference for pubic hair to you? With you, he can only have a serious discussion on art. After all, you are his daughter's friend.'

Pratap ran after me holding a kitchen knife. 'Tell me where your pubic hair is and I'll cut it off right away.'

We were new to Delhi at the time. Pooja and Pratap's so-called love story was rather unusual and to some extent mysterious. Brajesh Bhai had met Pratap at the opening of some exhibition. He found the boy smart, handsome and talented. At the show, the jury had placed one of Pratap's paintings in the 'Special Mention' category. This was Pratap's first introduction to the Delhi art circle. Brajesh Bhai, who inaugurated the show, had arrived with Pooja. She was a print maker. She wasn't all that beautiful, but was certainly attractive.

Evidently, Brajesh Bhai had secretly marked Pratap as

his son-in-law at their very first meeting. Pratap said: 'Try to understand, Ballubhai. I have landed in Delhi from a backward area. To create my space here I'll have to do a lot many things. Brajesh Bhai is influential and has a good image and vast contacts. He is a useful man. And even though he is an artist of the bygone era, he quite follows the art business.'

I reminded Pratap of the blurb of a short-story collection of my favourite Lucknow poet and writer, Kunwar Narayan, where he introduced himself by stating: 'I am in the automobile business so I won't have to go into the business of literature.'

'But Ballubhai, I don't have an automobile business. So, if I don't go into the art business, these people will swallow me up. I'm a realist. I nurse dreams. Who doesn't want to be successful?'

One day, Brajesh Bhai, accompanied by Pooja, ran into Pratap at an exhibition. He invited Pratap to his house, where a grand welcome awaited him. Pooja's mother bent over backwards to appease Pratap. Brajesh Bhai took out a bottle of Hungarian red wine. It was raining outside. In the porch, Pooja was sitting on a swing. Her large eyes had entranced Pratap. He slowly sipped the wine and concentrated his gaze on Pooja, while Brajesh Bhai was immersed in a long conversation on the phone.

On his return home, Pratap confided in me: 'Ballubhai, this is my first love, and perhaps my first dream.'

'But every affair is a first love for you. Anyway, what's this first dream?'

'Listen, I am being serious. Don't start laughing. It's a matter of life and death.'

'Okay, okay. Now tell me your dream.'

'Nothing much, Ballubhai. It's a simple dream.'

'Well, Brajesh Bhai has lots of property and she's his only daughter. So you don't really have to have any dreams. You're getting everything on a platter.'

'Come on, Ballubhai. Learn to think big. His property means nothing to me. I have a bigger and grander dream.'

'Now will you stop boring me? Just tell me what your dream is. Don't spin a yarn about it.'

'Well, my dream is to perform cunnilingus on Pooja. It's an intoxicating dream. That there's a lot of honey smeared between her legs and I am licking it madly.'

'You bloody pervert… So this is your dream?'

'Ballubhai, this is my real dream. But you won't understand. She looked like a divine beauty on the swing. The bloody red wine reminded me of Matisse's red.'

One day, Pratap was sitting in the front seat next to Brajesh Bhai in the car. Pooja was in the back. Brajesh Bhai was to visit a dentist in Sarojini Nagar. He told Pratap: 'Both of you chat up in the car. Why should you get bored watching whining patients at the dentist's? I'd be back soon.'

Pratap was quite nervous as he waited in the car. He wanted to say 'I love you' to Pooja, but realized he had to come up with the confession in a prim and proper manner. After all, it was to be the historic confession of a great artist of the future. But he was unable to figure out how he should go about it. It was rather risky to relate to her his cunnilingus dream at this first and somewhat private meeting. Most likely, she wouldn't even have understood the confession. It would be difficult to explain the meaning of cunnilingus to her.

The clock was ticking, but there was no dialogue. Brajesh Bhai could appear any time. And soon enough, there he was, approaching the car at a slow pace, his right hand pressed against his cheek.

This is a rare opportunity, which must not be allowed to pass. Tell her what's in your heart, Pratap rationalized. Brajesh Bhai was now quite close to the car.

'Poojaji...'

'Yes, Pratapji... Anything important? Why are you so nervous?'

'No, no. I'm not nervous. Actually, I wanted to tell you something.'

'Say it then. Once Papa is here, you won't be able to say anything.'

Before Brajesh Bhai could open the door, Pratap rattled off: 'You see, Pooja, I have a crush on you.'

That evening, I had a long chat with Pratap. 'Listen, Pratap, in love you should straight away say "I love you". What's this crush business? She may not have even followed you.'

Around this time, Pratap took to visiting Brajesh Bhai at his house every Sunday evening. Those were the days Doordarshan would screen popular Hindi films on Sundays. Our Godard and Fellini fan took to watching them with a kind of religious fervour. Pooja's mother would prepare a hearty dinner for Pratap. His routine would be to keep staring at Pooja between spells of concentrating on the film. But most of his interaction would be with Pooja's mother. On such occasions, Brajesh Bhai would often disappear for a long walk. Sometimes, Pratap would also try to get up and would say: 'Shall I also come with you, sir?'

'Come on, what will you do walking alongside this old man? Enjoy the movie. Why don't you discuss art with Pooja sometimes? She talks sparingly, contrary to her mum.' At this point, the mum would start muttering inaudibly. But Pooja's large eyes would keep Pratap spellbound.

This cycle lasted about ten months. But there was no progress whatsoever on making a clear-cut confession of love. One day, a frustrated Pratap told me: 'Ballubhai, would you call this a love affair? I am bored to death watching those third-rate Hindi films. So much so that as I watched Godard's *Breathless* at Alliance Française the other day, I suddenly had this feeling that I was in the wrong cinema hall. I was unable to watch it. Just think about my future...'

I couldn't help smiling. 'Looks like you've forgotten your honey-licking dream. Carry on, Pratap. The journey's end is not very far.'

'One shouldn't tell you anything. But I'll say one thing. I am not going to Pooja's house to watch the movie this Sunday. Remembers The Doors song '*This is the end*'? Enough!'

And true to his word, Pratap disappeared the following Sunday. God knows where he went. Brajesh Bhai's house was not very far. He sent across his servant with a message that everybody was waiting for Pratap and the dinner was ready.

Finally, he invited me instead. Perhaps I was destined to have dinner at their house that night. And I did it ample justice. The film of the day was Bhagwan Dada's *Albela*, and I enjoyed that too. To hell with Godard! Here was our cinema and our hero. Geeta Bali looked so sexy swinging to the song '*Shola jo bhadke*'!

That day, I lectured Pratap for a long time, telling him that if he delayed it any longer, he'd find himself in a bind. 'You must strike while the iron is hot. But you seem to be running away from the situation.'

'Ballubhai, I really cannot figure out what to do.'

'What is there to do? Just write her a straight and simple love letter. In fact, just bluntly write:"I love you, Pooja". Don't include any of your intellectual nonsense and you'll soon find yourself the son-in-law of a wealthy family. Your career will also take off. Pooja is a nice girl. Those fancy-free intellectual girls are not meant to be housewives.'

Pratap went into his thinking mode. 'Okay, Ballubhai. I'll write a love letter tomorrow. The matter must be taken forward. I haven't even kissed her yet. I have nothing to show for my ten months of effort. Really shameful. Why, I have begun to hate myself! I'm a bloody coward!'

'Then go ahead and unfurl the flag of your bravery tomorrow. Don't delay any further.'

Eventually, Pratap did write the letter, but it's deeply saddening to say that it was not addressed to Pooja, but to Brajesh Bhai. This was it:

'Respected Brajesh Bhai, my respectful salutations. I have been meaning to write this letter to you for quite some time. For the last few days, I have been under a lot of pressure from many quarters. My father continues to pester me in his letters from Gorakhpur that I should now settle down. He says that after looking at my birth chart, an astrologer has declared that my career will take off only after Goddess Lakshmi comes into the house. He has even found a beautiful and decent girl for me. He's only waiting for my consent. I don't want to hide anything from you. In Delhi you offered me a far better environment than I ever had even at home. My father, Devdutt Rastogi, is a schoolteacher. He teaches maths, but I am quite scared of the subject. He doesn't understand what dreams a true artist nourishes. My mother passed away soon after my birth. Indeed, like M.F. Husain, I also never got to see my mother's face. My father consigned all her photographs to Mother Ganga. He never remarried and raised me with a lot of affection. But the very mention of maths was enough to send me to bed with high fever. Up to the fifth standard, my father would often punish me over this issue. Then gradually, it dawned on him that his son was fated to become an artist. For him, this career meant financial struggle, aimlessness and a sort of madness. But one day, I drew a nice, large portrait of him, had it framed and very formally hung it in the drawing room, which brought him a lot of happiness.

'I realize there's no need for me to tell you all this. I must come to the point. I understand that both you and your wife are fully aware that I like Pooja. Rather, my friend Baldev believes both of you wish us to fall in love and settle down. He often asks me why an eminent painter should come down to our flat to give me driving lessons. Why does your family wait for me so eagerly every Sunday?

'I am unable to make out to whom I should address my letter. Pooja is an artist too, but I feel I should first open up my heart to you. Sometimes, I find her to be quite childlike. I feel awkward addressing a letter to her. That's why I am writing to you instead. I feel that you alone can resolve my dilemma. Yours, Pratap.'

Pratap showed the letter to me before giving it to Brajesh

Bhai. I vehemently told him to not hand it to Brajesh Bhai. I also had a long argument with him, saying that while he claimed to be a follower of John Berger and had studied serious works, his letter was written in the language of an ordinary boy and with sentiments and emotions only an ordinary person was capable of having. I also advised him to write a straightforward letter to Pooja instead.

The great sculptor Ramkinkar would often tell a story: When Rabindranath Tagore was on his death bed, he called over Kinkar Da to his bedside and said: 'Whatever you see, don't give it up. Catch it by the throat. Don't let go of it until you've got full control over it. And once it comes under your control, don't look back.' Samaresh Basu made this particular episode the basis of his novel on Ramkinkar's life and named it *Dekhi Nai Phire (Never Look Back)*.

Pratap said to me: 'Ballubhai, your advice makes sense and I am now wondering what to do with this letter.' But he finally handed it to Brajesh Bhai. The following day, Brajesh Bhai did come down to give the driving lesson, but remained silent about the letter. Instead, he rambled on about how a driver should be careful on the road when schoolchildren were around. Finally, he indicated that, 'It's something between you and Pooja. But your letter makes it appear as if my wife and I are working on some plan to make you fall in love with each other.'

Brajesh Bhai was to leave for Poland the very next day, so the driving lessons were interrupted. Pratap too gradually emerged from the emotional shock. Thereafter, for many days, he immersed himself in Beethoven's Ninth instead.

Many years later, I was visiting Brajesh Bhai on his

sick bed. Pooja was happily married by then. Brajesh Bhai inquired about Pratap. 'I am told he is quite a celebrity now. But I'll give you some sage advice. If you ever feel like writing a love letter to a girl, never ever make the mistake of addressing it to her father instead.'

'But I am already married, sir.' I was somewhat flustered. There was no point telling Pratap this. He had moved on and had taken the expression 'Never look back' to the other extreme.

Car, Action and
Mr Ten Per Cent

The year 2007 is a landmark in the Indian art world. The preceding five years had created an unusual, almost surreal, milieu and the number of art galleries had risen at an alarmingly fast pace. The basements in south Delhi alone comprised of a number of galleries. It was a time when collectors, investors and gallery owners fiercely competed with each other to lay hands on canvases. By this time, the top rung artists had gone beyond their grasp, which meant the artists in the A and A+ categories were no longer to be had. If anything, there was the danger of only their fakes turning up in the market. All eyes were now set on what was left of the 'B' category stalwarts.

Many young and talked-about (there were numerous stories about why they were talked about in the first place) artists were busy to the point of being overstretched and had given up discussing art issues altogether. If four of Delhi's hottest young artists got together at a fashion designer's cocktail party, their main topic of discussion would be,

'Which car would be the best buy?' One young painter, far from being excited about art, was obsessed with cars. The fashion designer host put his hand on a hottie's shoulder and said: 'Would you please book four of your 4 x 4 canvases for me? And don't try to play a fast one on me.'

'Honestly, I have nothing to offer. Why don't you come down to my studio and check it out for yourself? I don't have a single work ready. Only empty frames lying around. I haven't even stretched the canvas on them. As you know, I don't have an assistant. I have a unique style and if someone else barely even touches up my work, its meaning will be altered.'

The fashion designer smiled and pressed the artist's shoulder: 'All right, book four empty frames for me and paint them in your own time.'

Art market guerrillas were busy chalking out ever-new strategies in this situation. Somewhere, there was a list of sick, about-to-kick-the-bucket artists. I remember watching at Alliance Française a feature film on Modigliani's life, where the day before his death, a gallery owner landed up at his door to buy up all his works.

I'll now relate the story of two so-called about-to-die painters. I know about them, because in those days, I would scout for such artists on Asha Sahay's behalf. My survival in Delhi now depended not so much on painting anything, but on the 10 per cent commission I earned as a middleman for other painters. Why, one collector would even address me as 'Mister Ten Per Cent'!

Pratap still remains in coma and doctors have more or less given up on him. As I sit in the hospital waiting room, I can recall two such cases.

A young art collector (whose father was a big-time builder) met me at a party one day. He dragged me into a corner and asked: 'Baldevbhai, what do you think of Balraj Taneja?'

'Well, he is a good painter. I heard he has not been keeping well for quite some time. The poor guy is close to 80 and life has been a struggle for him. But his work is really good.'

'I heard you are on the jury of a big award given by the Madhya Pradesh government. I want you to make sure Taneja is given the award this year. In return, I am prepared to buy one of your paintings right away.'

'But why are you showing so much affection for him? He is alone, a bachelor and bedridden... Why are you so keen on his work?'

'If you ask me, I'm very keen. Next week, I'm going to buy his entire lifetime's work. I've even given him an advance. I won't leave behind even one work hanging in his studio.'

'Then I have some advice for you. You better send a truck today itself. Mehta is also looking to cut a deal with him. And take out your cheque-book. The prices of my paintings are also going up fast. I am no longer Ten Per Cent, but Sixty Per Cent.'

All of Balraj Taneja's artwork was picked up that night. My painting also sold for a good price. I immediately made my sulking landlord happy. I hadn't paid him for a year. You must be wondering what happened to Taneja. Given his condition, what could he do with so much cash, especially since he had no next of kin?

Yet, what transpired was hilarious. Soon after the deal was through, he recovered completely and bought a huge car with ample room to load canvases. He also purchased a large amount of art material. After all, it was necessary to continue to work now. The studio had been emptied and he had raised his rates overnight. Alas, despite my best efforts, I couldn't get him the award; another member was hell bent on pushing a bigger name.

The poor collector, who had cleared out his studio, was both astonished and crestfallen, wondering what magical potion had brought Taneja back to life. In fact, he confessed as much: 'The amazing thing is, my chemist told me that the other day Taneja had come to him looking for Viagra! It's a miracle! And I was under the impression that his days were numbered!'

Even today, in 2010, Balraj Taneja is doing fine, working hard, and his creative juices have assumed a new course. His bulk-buyer is at his wit's end, since the market is flooded with his new works. But he is pinning hopes on the fact that since all his old works are in his stock, he is bound to make a profit one day.

Girdharilal's case is even more entertaining. He was counted among the top-rung painters at one time. Over the years, his children settled abroad, his wife passed away, and he had no financial worries either. But nearly all his work lay unsold. Things changed in the last year. He began to suffer from health issues and even had to be admitted to the ICU a couple of times. Ever since she learnt this, Asha Sahay was after me to help her cut a good deal for Girdharilal's entire work. She was aware that another powerful party was working on the same lines.

'How much are they offering?' I asked Asha Sahay.

'They are willing to shell out two crores. Imagine, until two years ago, no one was willing to pay even ten thousand for his work. It's the opportunity of a lifetime and you'll earn a handsome commission.'

I went down to Girdharilal's studio. He was actually very sick and was babbling away in a state of high fever. Only his houseboy, who knew me, was around.

'Where are the saheb's paintings?'

'Everything is lying locked up in the studio. Tiwariji had come. He has instructed me that no one is to even touch those works. He is the one bearing all his medical expenses.'

'Who's this Tiwari? Never heard of him.'

'He claims to be a big businessman. Says he'll set up a museum in the saheb's village named after him. Saheb also likes him a lot.'

'How much is he getting for the entire lot?'

'I don't know the details, but I guess four crore. But Saheb hasn't agreed yet.'

Girdharilal called over the houseboy; it was time for some water and medicines. I sat down by his bedside and touched his feet. He continued to stare at me, as if trying to place me.

'I see, so you are Baldev,' he said, finally recognizing me after much effort. 'Pratap has really achieved unimaginable success.' He was virtually dragging his words out.

'Sir, you better think about your health. Pratap no longer belongs to our circle of artists.'

Whatever Girdharilal uttered were the babblings of a person in the grip of high fever. Then suddenly he gripped my arm. 'How would the silver colour look?'

'Amazing, sir! Even in this condition you are thinking about colours! You have always used silver in your works very effectively. I admire you.'

The houseboy whispered to me: 'Tiwari is buying saheb a car and he is referring to the choice of colour for that. He has sought my opinion too and once asked me, "Will black be okay?" But I told him that a black car would be invisible in the dark.'

I sat there, reflecting over the situation, when all of a sudden, Girdharilal sat up and appeared to be in deep thought. I recalled the days when, after a party, he'd drop me home on his second-hand scooter.

Then as suddenly, he fell back and again began to babble: 'I think a silver Honda would be all right. The delivery is due on Friday. Tiwari appears to be an honest man.'

By chance, Tiwari arrived while I was still with Girdharilal. He handed the houseboy a massive lock to put on the studio door. Then he sat down on the floor by Girdharilal's bed and began to whisper something into his ear. Had he come to give Girdharilal the papers for the car?

As I stepped out of Girdharilal's house that evening, I couldn't help recall the scene in Satyajit Ray's *Shatranj Ke Khiladi*, where two players land up at a dying nawab's house to play chess. And then they try to leave precipitately; the nawab is dead and all one can hear is the plaintive shrieks of the ladies of the harem. I faced a similar situation. I wasn't walking, I was trying to escape. I had this illusion that Girdharilal had left this world and his houseboy was crying in grief.

This happened three years ago, but Girdharilal is fit as a fiddle even today. If the fancy grips him, he also gets down to painting, and at least once a week, goes out for a spin in his silver Honda. In his moments of forced idleness, his chauffeur sometimes wonders what's so magical about the red-and-black blobs squiggled by the saheb that he prices them in lakhs. In those moments, he can't help telling the houseboy: 'I am sure he is a liar. He is not fully fit yet and has become eccentric.'

The houseboy's riposte is interesting: 'Bastard, I know that you pour four spoons of sugar in your tea... I won't give you more than two next time. Even I have come down to one, so you too better mend your ways.' Tiwari's big lock is hanging outside the studio door. The houseboy is unable to explain why Tiwari hasn't called up in the last one year. 'Earlier he'd phone virtually every day.'

In Delhi, I appreciated only one art critic—Prabhat Shankar Agnihotri—who, for a number of years, wrote under the pseudonym 'Arteye'. He would often reminisce about the days when art critics like Charles Fabri and Richard Bartholomew were held in high esteem, were names to reckon with in the Delhi art circles and had a vision all their own.

Prabhat Shankar had regularly contributed on art in a leading newspaper for a decade. But in 2005, he was sacked summarily and disgracefully and his highly popular column was handed over to a wealthy businessman's 'cultured' wife, Manjula.

Even more humiliating was the fact that he was thrown out not by the editor, but by the newspaper's brand manager. Just a few years earlier, the manager would greet him most politely with folded hands. But he had become so powerful that now editors were forced to stand in front of him in that same posture.

When Prabhat Shankar entered the brand manager's cabin, he was not even asked to take a seat. The manager straight away told him: 'I've learnt you quite like drinking...'

'Yes, I do.'

'I've also learnt that you only go to those art shows where liquor is served. And that often you even demand a bottle in return for a good review.'

'That's a lie!' Prabhat Shankar shot back angrily. 'It's rubbish! There was a time when an art critic by the name of Raina would demand a bottle from big galleries and he'd get it too. The gallery managers of those days would proudly boast that they could even get hold of a work by an eminent artist like Sailoz Mukherjea in return for a bottle of rum. But these are all anecdotes of the art world. Raina was given the bottle because the paper he worked for was read in the diplomatic circles and he wielded certain power on account of his writings.'

'You are blowing your top for no reason, Agnihotri Saheb. You choose to go to only those shows where liquor is in ample supply. It's not a made-up story, it's a fact. And you even have a code word to find out whether a party would serve liquor or not.'

'What do you want to say? Why don't you come out straight? I'm aware that to grab hold of my column, Manjula has fed all manner of misinformation to you. And what's this code word? All my life I have written on art with complete honesty and sincerity. You have no right to spoil my reputation in this manner.'

'Then, let me tell you Agnihotri Saheb, your code word is "Action". You inquire with the party at the other end whether there's any action or not...'

Prabhat Shankar was left speechless. He would sometimes certainly ask his bosom pals: 'Would there be any action?' In an expansive mood, he would occasionally even add: '*Bol Radha bol*, action *hoga ki nahin*' paraphrasing a famous old Bollywood song.

How dare a two-penny brand manager speak to him in this tone? He left the cabin in a huff. In the evening, he was at my studio and, in the middle of our conversation, began to cry. He was an honest man, knew the history of art like the back of his hand and was conversant with all the techniques of painting. And while he liked to drink, it never influenced his writings or opinions. Not even one per cent. He had a great sense of humour and had a characteristic manner of pronouncing the word 'action'.

At a seminar at Max Mueller Bhavan, he had made a controversial statement that the cultural circles of Delhi were under the thrall of a bunch of culture-vulture type wives of the moneyed members of society, who moved about in limousines, but hardly cared to go through any serious works on art. His comment did not refer to all the women; indeed, he had also pointed out a handful of competent and cultured critics among them.

But during the lunch that followed, this set of culture-vultures declared war on him. Manjula too came down on him like a ton of bricks: 'What's your problem if my husband is rich? You may fancy getting pushed about in DTC buses, but I have a car, a chauffeur, and all the time in the world. Moreover, we don't hanker after any "action" either...'

So, it was clear who had instructed the brand manager. After losing his column, Prabhat Shankar busied himself with a book. But he had been deeply hurt. He passed away in 2007. There were barely half a dozen artists at the crematorium and hardly any other people. When his body was brought in, flies buzzed all over it and his younger daughter was trying to fan them away.

In the evening, I sat alone in my studio, raised a glass, and in fond memory of the departed soul said: 'Action!'

Then there was this phone call that I received from a gallery: 'We've heard that Prabhat Shankar had some really good paintings in his collection. Do you know his daughters? We can come to some arrangement. Please get in touch with them and you'll also make some cash.'

I was already in a foul mood, so I concocted a lie: 'Yes, I had spoken to his younger daughter about his collection. She doesn't want to sell anything. In fact, she told me that his collection was all that was left of her father's memory.'

I realize there are corrupt art critics too out there. They drink, they cohabit with under-teens (yes, this is a little different from consorting with teenagers)and do much more. But placing Prabhat Shankar in their category would be insulting art itself. When he said 'action', it had an altogether different meaning. Action, for him, meant a congenial and serious discussion after drinks. This is what he meant by cocktail culture.

One day, a fixer-cum-artist by the name of Navratna Pandey called him over to his house party. Liquor, food and all 'other personal conveniences' were available. Pandey was a crafty character of average talent. At parties, one often noticed him sucking up to the art critics, massaging their egos, extending them invitations and organizing taxis, etc., for them. He offered homage to everyone without discrimination. An old art institution of Delhi had at one time given him a big award. He had put their shield on display right in the middle of his studio. His house was somewhere on the fringes of Janakpuri, but he had rented a flat in a government colony and in that so-called studio, he would throw his colourful parties.

He had tried to invite Prabhat Shankar on numerous occasions, but Prabhat couldn't stand him. In those days, Prabhat was a member of an important jury. One day, Navratna Pandey landed up at his house in a cab and cajoled him into coming along. Immediately on arrival at his studio, he played his cards. 'Prabhat sir, I have very high regard for you. But who doesn't need cash these days? I know a big businessman's wife, who has to her credit some excellent work in abstract. Really impressive. It won fulsome praise at a Paris exhibition. If you get her an award, it'll bring rewards for all of us. The award is worth one lakh, out of which you can keep 50,000. She doesn't need any money; her husband is filthy rich.'

Prabhat Shankar stared continuously at Pandey for some time. So much so, soon Pandey grew nervous. Then Prabhat began to hoot with laughter and slapped Pandey on the shoulder. 'Yaar Pandey, you don't know my fee. If you want to buy me, then at least give me my price. Tell her I want a good brand of car.'

For a moment, Pandey was stunned. What had happened to Prabhat Shankar? Was he being serious or was he pulling his leg? Then he too began to laugh: 'Sir, I really enjoyed today. You are a wonderful talker. Your message shall be conveyed.'

I heard that one day, Pandey had called over some 'fast' girls to his studio to look after the VIPs. But an alert neighbour informed the police. When his flat was raided, Pandey tried to impress policemen with the shield. 'The president had given me this award.'

'And did he also give you the permit to run a den of prostitutes in a government flat, Mr Pandey?'

As a consequence, Pandey had to serve time in jail. Now, whenever we meet, he is quite sheepish. But he did turn up at Prabhat Shankar's funeral. I was surprised. He said: 'He was a very good man, sir. Honest and upright.'

'And the best thing is, he was an "action lover" too,' I said, trying to lighten the atmosphere.

The Final Chapter

The arrival of Pratap's father from Gorakhpur had all of a sudden added immensely to my responsibilities. He had known me since the early days of my association with his son. Seeing the old man in his hour of need, I completely changed my resolve. All I knew was that after Pratap's amazing success, he had stopped visiting Delhi. Even after Pratap went into coma, it took him a fortnight to arrive, as the news had reached him very late. Once in Delhi, I was the first person he contacted. I didn't tell him that Pratap and I had ceased to be friends for some years now.

I was in a dilemma. Looking at him, I could sense I might be in for a lot of running around. After Pratap had gone into a coma, I was driven to reflect over our 30-year association and tried to recall, judge, assess and understand the moments of our friendship. And a new perspective on his career, achievements and limitations began to evolve.

I also had to visit the hospital quite often. One afternoon, a Mrs Aruna Kasliwal approached me. She reeked of money and claimed that a collector was trying to sell her one of

Pratap's highly desirable paintings at a fancy price. I had never seen the original, but I had the catalogue of the New York exhibition that carried its photograph.

'I'd be grateful if you could give me that catalogue.' Mrs Kasliwal opened her purse and held out ten notes of 500 each.

'No, no. What is this? Why don't you have the catalogue photocopied? A good colour photocopy should do.' I was in a fix.

'No, it's a matter of being professional. I would like to buy this catalogue. Since I am buying such an expensive painting, I better have the original catalogue as well in my collection.'

'How much are you going to pay for the painting?' I asked, accepting the cash.

'Two crore.'

'Quite a bit.'

'Well, I am told it's Pratap's favourite work.'

'I believe he never sold his favourite works.'

'But I am going to have it.'

'Good luck to you.'

A week later, she invited me to her house and even sent a car to fetch me. When I arrived, she said: 'Baldev sir, please come to my bedroom. There's a surprise for you.'

And there indeed was a surprise. The catalogue painting was on the wall.

'Oh, great… So you finally own the painting.'

'Yes, once I set my heart on something, I don't give up until I possess it.'

I contemplated the painting. Its yellow background was quite luminous. Pratap's assistant couldn't have made it. Mrs

Kasliwal asked me to authenticate the work. She gave me one lakh rupees. All the papers were ready; I couldn't say no.

The next day, I learnt that Pratap had died at the hospital. He'd been in coma for 33 days. The electric crematorium was quite crowded. In a city where people hadn't come to know in time about the death of an artist of Gaitonde's stature, for the media of that city, the news of Pratap's death was something momentous. Nevertheless, I refused interviews by the press.

Pratap's father now handed over complete responsibility to me. He wanted all the money in Pratap's name to be used to set up a trust in his name. He even told me, in a calm and even voice, that he didn't want a single penny of it. 'I am comfortable in Gorakhpur. I can look after myself all my life. This kind of money will make me go crazy. I am good at maths, but keeping account of this kind of money will be mind-boggling even for me.'

My career as a painter was now over. But I felt it was possible to do some fruitful work in Pratap's memory. One could organize fellowships, and set up a library and other facilities for young painters. The trust was flush with funds and I felt my life had finally found a purpose.

As I entered Pratap's bedroom for the first time after his death, I was shocked to discover a large painting on the wall. It was the same painting Mrs Kasliwal had bought for two crore. But there was no luminous yellow here. Instead, it was an ochre yellow. Obviously, the catalogue image did not have the right shade. So the original was in Pratap's collection after all. I even had it examined by experts.

Then I phoned Mrs Kasliwal. Nobody picked up. I asked Pratap's driver to immediately take me to her house. There,

I found a security guard who told me: 'Sir, there is no entry from here at all… I was away in my village and returned only yesterday.'

'But I was shown a painting hanging in the bedroom. The colour of the door is also right. This is exactly where I had come.'

'No, sir, this house has been lying locked up for many days. I believe you are mistaken. It could have been another similar house.'

I felt giddy for a second, but somehow steadied myself. Then told the driver: 'Let's go. Take me home.'

'Where? To your home, sir?'

But where's my home? I was again feeling giddy.

Pratap, do you know where your home was?

Do I know where my home is?

P.S.

....

In Conversation with Vinod Bhardwaj
Brij Sharma

⋯⟨⟩ ⟨⟩⋯

Turning Approver for an Exciting,
Spicy, Poignant and Tragic World
Uday Prakash

⋯⟨⟩ ⟨⟩⋯

Insights
Interviews
& More...

What would you like to call yourself—poet, short-story writer, novelist, art critic or film critic? The range of your activities over the last 45 years has been rather versatile.

My father worked for the State Bank of India. It was previously called Imperial Bank and he had joined it in the pre-Partition Lahore. But even before the Partition he had himself transferred to Lucknow. My elder brother was born in Lahore whereas I was born in Lucknow. At home there was not much of an atmosphere to inspire one to become a writer, but my father was quite fond of reading the novels of Tagore and Saratchandra. The latter's *Datta* was among his favourites. When I became active in the world of literary writing at Lucknow's Kanyakubj College, I would take pains to hide my Punjabi background from my peers. Every year, during the two months of summer vacations, my mother would leave for her village of Bahalpur near Hoshiarpur in Punjab to see her parents. I would also go with her and live in the village. But I would never tell my literary friends that

121

I was a Punjabi. And while at home, until well past my teens I would speak to my mother in Punjabi, to my friends I would say I had no village to go back to, that we were city-dwellers.

Once a huge trunk arrived from Lahore in my father's name and I distinctly remember it contained a knife among other objects. Years later I wrote a short story, 'Chaku', about it. The point is that on one side, there were blood-stained memories rooted in the Partition narratives related by family members and on the other, a strange feeling of a kind of backwardness owing to my Punjabi origins as I moved in literary circles. In Lucknow I had many Muslim friends. When I joined Lucknow University, in no time some of the nationally-known artists and Hindi writers became my close friends. Eminent printmaker Jai Krishna Agrawal ran the graphics department at the arts college in those days. Naresh Saxena was a well-known Hindi poet. We brought out a small magazine focusing on poetry and the arts titled *Aarambh*, which transformed my world.

Jai Krishna's first wife Gogi Sarojpal was a sort of rebellious painter whose uncle Yashpal was an eminent Hindi writer and revolutionary. Thanks to Jai Krishna I came in contact with many big names among artists and started to write on art. Those were the days when I was quite taken by Gogi's persona. At the time Gyanpith Award-winning writer Kunwar Narayan's house *Vishnukuti* in Mahanagar was a leading rendezvous for India's eminent faces on the cultural scene. It was a house where personalities like Agyeya, Birju Maharaj, Amir Khan Saheb, Pandit Jasraj, B.V. Karanth, Raghuvir Sahay and Sanjukta Panigrahi would come and stay. Kunwar Narayan was 21 years older to me, but we became friends. I could go to his house and stay in the guest room, and was free to use his vast library any time. My world swung between the British Council Library and *Vishnukuti*.

Around this time I also started writing on cinema after having watched some of the best films made in Europe. My poems and short stories began to appear in magazines. Dhumil from Benares was quite a name in Hindi poetry at that time. He would often visit Lucknow to push for his transfer out of Saharanpur and would stay with me. Indeed all my friends were at least eight years older to me.

Joining the weekly *Dinmaan* published by the *Times of India* was a dream for every young writer in those days. Its editor was the eminent Hindi poet Raghuvir Sahay who began to commission me to write on art, cinema, modern thought and so on. While I was doing M.A. in Psychology, I once received a telegram from Raghuvir Sahai asking me to immediately send him a write-up on Chomsky. In other words, at a young age itself, I had become an elderly figure. In my *Aarambh* days, I was merely a student, but many writers believed I was some middle-aged professor.

Of course you are quite familiar with my year-long training in journalism in 1973 at *Dharmyug* published by *The Times of India*. We started our career from the three-seater room in the National Hostel where one bed was occupied by you.

In those days you were eager to join Dinmaan *in Delhi whereas Dharmvir Bharati,* Dharmyug *editor and the writer of the landmark play* Andha Yug, *wanted to make sure you settled down in Bombay.*

In those days all of us considered the position of a sub editor in *Dinmaan* as prestigious as a professorship at the Jawaharlal Nehru University. But I had a great time during the one year spent in Bombay in the company of S.P. Singh and M.J. Akbar. Udayan Sharma was my flatmate in a luxury flat on Napean Sea Road. On Sundays we would often go to Akbar's flat in the Chand Society in Juhu. Akbar and Mallika were in the middle of their affair in those days. Subsequently the three of them rose to become eminent figures in the world of Hindi and English journalism. Indeed initially, after he had left *The Illustrated Weekly of India*, Akbar wrote a number of letters to me. At the time he was quite taken by the *Dinmaan* style of journalism. Once I finally succeeded in joining *Dinmaan* in Delhi in 1974, I had ample opportunities to freely write on art and cinema.

Back then even the leading artists had no airs about them. One could easily make friends with them, whether it was Husain, Souza, Swaminathan, Manjit Bawa, Arpita Singh, A. Ramachandran or Ram Kumar. Souza wrote a string of historically-significant letters to me from New York. Manjit Bawa would drive me home at night from Garhi on his ramshackle scooter. I also managed to interview major filmmakers like Roman Polansky and Janussi. In Delhi my close friendship with poet and critic Vishnu Khare turned out to be a decisive phase in my life. He had just returned after a sojourn in Czechoslovakia and had a good collection of western classical music records. We bonded over our common love for the western classical music. I was lucky to have made friends with so many eminent personalities.

You were better known for your poetry at the time. You received the Bharat Bhushan Agrawal Prize which even today is a highly recognized honour.

At that time poetry was considered the key aspect of literature. But in the beginning I also wrote some short stories which were published in literary journals. But more than writers, I liked to spend my evenings in the company of artists and sculptors sitting in their studios. My book *Adhunik Kala Kosh* (Encylopaedia of Modern Art) became so popular among the young artists of Bihar that it continued to be photocopied. When artist Subodh

124

Sketch of Vinod Bhardwaj by internationally known Indian artist Subodh Gupta

125

Gupta—quite a name today—landed in Delhi in the early 1990s, he directly came to the *Dinmaan* offices carrying the transparencies of his paintings.

Where did you get this inspiration to suddenly publish a novel after crossing the age of 60? And now you are even planning a trilogy with the first novel on an artist, the second on a journalist and the third on a sex addict.

I have always been writing short stories and some years ago my collection called *Chiteri* came out. But I had never thought of writing a novel. In the Hindi world autobiographies and biographies are normally written after much deliberation and with great care. It's a particular kind of fake truth. I quite agree with Hemingway's statement that 'people in a novel, not skilfully constructed characters, must be projected from the writer's assimilated experience, from his knowledge, from his head, from his heart and from all there is of him'. Which means that in the case of a character in a novel, his world too is to be based to a great extent on experienced reality heavy with autobiographical overtones.

The world of art as I saw it initially, i.e. after 1968, was quite different. Back then, art was not a bazaar at all. The painters either taught or followed some other pursuits. And it was an amazing experience going to their studios, sitting and chatting with them and watching them at work. During an evening with Swaminathan even an ordinary peg of rum would open up uncommon doors of perception. In the course of his intense creative impulsion when Souza managed to complete seven canvases in one day, to see him and discuss art changed the entire world of theories. Chatting with Jogen Chowdhury in the corridors of Rashtrapati Bhavan or at his home gave a new insight into viewing and perceiving things. When Manjit Bawa, in his Sufi ebullience, would start singing on a visit to my house, he created a heavenly atmosphere. But gradually the art mart began to give an obscene shape to artists' thoughts, lifestyle, relations and attitude. Inside a fashion designer's hot spot gallery, four talented painters sat discussing not art but who had bought which brand of car.

Between 2001 and 2008, the kind of obscene atmosphere the Indian art bazaar managed to create was far worse than anything the West had known. Tyeb Mehta rightly pointed out in the course of one interview that while we had absorbed all the bad elements of the western art world, we had adopted none of their good qualities. The night Manjit Bawa passed into a coma—for a long time it turned out—that evening I had seen him at a gallery's inaugural party. He looked quite tense. His face was covered in sweat. He left early. I didn't realize then that he was leaving for ever. For all his friends, his lapsing into a coma was terribly bad news. After a few days, while he was still in the hospital, I noticed his photograph in the colour pages of one of capital's leading dailies. It showed him holding a glass of wine with a pretty face by his side. The person who had written the caption wasn't even aware that the artist was lying in a hospital fighting for his life. Subrata Kundu, a lesser-known artist used to be a regular hero at the Page Three parties in the capital. He lost a leg in a horrific accident and was subsequently conspicuous as an unwelcome guest at glamorous galleries going about on crutches wearing an abject look. No paper carried the news of his death. Nor was the death of an artist of the stature of Gaitonde news for the Press. Today when his works are exhibited at Guggenheim Museum in New York, it tickles the connoisseurs of Indian art no end. And you notice in the art circles many a rich woman in sexy attire, a glass of wine in

Sketch of Vinod Bhardwaj by internationally known Indian artist Subodh Gupta

hand, trying to make laughable attempts at appreciating 'Gai' and 'Swami'.

The assistants to the artists on the make moved around complaining of low wages and virtually no perks. The Indian art bazaar at this time had a surrealist atmosphere. Some mysterious character would be running around frenetically with a suitcase packed with 10 to 15 million rupees to lay hands on a work by some eminent painter. The universe of my novel is aimed at finding and analyzing a ruthless truth. Initially I wrote three chapters; then I filed them away and forgot about them. Three years later, I didn't even look at the old draft, but started to write anew. And this time around I finished the work. Even now a lot of young artists – some of them callow youth – come to me to buy the Hindi version of the novel. They came in a gang once, seemingly promising young artists. One of them was a carpenter's son, another's father worked in a coal mine. One of them had also been an assistant to a big-time artist. These are the readers who have true empathy for my novel. Not only do they read the novel themselves, they persuade others to read it as well. It's like a virus.

Your novel must have alienated some artists, gallery owners, party gatecrashers...

In India, the language of modern art is English. The English translation will be read by many more people and will also sell more than the Hindi edition. Maybe some people will be upset with it. I recall a story about Orhan Pamuk. His mother stopped talking to him after reading his *Istanbul*. The point is a writer does not write to please his friends, relatives or readers. This trilogy is not going to spare even me, so how can the others escape?

Nowadays a degree of sanity has crept back into the art bazaar. How do you feel about it? Does that create the possibility of writing another novel about the art world?

When players like Shahid Afridi or Virender Sehwag got out in the wake of a quick succession of sixers on a cricket field, the game did experience a kind of sanity. But the madness of the art bazaar is far more surreal than surrealism itself. It's not unlikely that once my trilogy is complete I will once again find myself lost in the maze of the stories and anecdotes of the world of art. Borges once said, 'I no longer want to write on tigers, mazes, mirrors etc. Why should I imitate my imitators?' But many doors of the art world still remain unopened. For the present, there is no need for imitation. A lady who runs a famous gallery once said, 'People claim that after drugs, dealing in art is the most powerful profession.' There's a lot more in this world that is yet be known and explored.

In a way *Seppuku* is a sting operation involving the Delhi art world. It presents episodes spanning the global art market of the eighties, and the nineties and the fearful bursting of the international corporate balloon just five years ago in the form of disparate stories and anecdotes put together as an exciting collage. Indeed it is a stunning albeit an authentic exposé of Delhi's art underworld. Somewhat like Bhikhu Mhatre of *Satya* exposing one by one the layers of the Bombay mafia's bloody intrigues and rivalries.

You may call *Seppuku* a novel or a string of disparate episodes in the manner of talented Polish storyteller Bruno Schulz' *The Street of Crocodiles*, but it remains an unusual collection of stories involving an unsuccessful artist's desperate confessions—apparently disparate but actually expanding and merging into each other. A Hindi scholar might consign it to the same 'litporn' category where he has pigeonholed Ugra, Ismat Chughtai, Manto and more recently Manohar Shyam Joshi's novella *Humzaad*—the same *Humzaad* which in recent times has been the first

131

work of Hindi fiction to muster the courage to explore the underbelly of Bollywood in considerable detail. Just as *Humzaad* is a fictional narration of the black money flowing into the production of pop cinema in Bollywood and the rise and fall of the obscene and corrupt 'culture' based on the despicable riches generated from the underworld wealth, *Seppuku* relates the tales of human tragedies and poignant dilemmas originating in the filth, cut-throat competition, trickeries and frauds engulfing the Capital's art bazaar with the swift pace of a newspaper reporter.

You must recall that just as *Humzaad's* old protagonist Topandas Khilluram Narkani suffocates to death in a luxury hotel between the thighs of a girl while in the throes of performing cunnilingus, the filthy rich 'successful' artists in *Seppuku*, sick of the surfeit of luxury yet in pursuit of more intense 'kicks' of pleasure, convert the noble and elite world of art into a shamelessly meandering gutter enlivened by the likes of Mastram or Savita Bhabhi. As you read *Seppuku*, you are sometimes reminded of the naturalist fiction of the early 20th century, which tended to focus on the recklessly obscene world populated by the European and Russian nobility.

Vinod Bhardwaj has been constantly moving between the worlds of art and literature for many years. Since he is an established art critic, it has been possible for him to transform the reality behind the frenetic world of the art mart into fictional narratives which otherwise would have gone unnoticed—at least in the world of Hindi fiction. These tales have come out of the pen of an art critic and poet-storyteller who has explored the world beyond Bartholomew, Geeta Kapur, Swaminathan and our endearing art-ideologue Sunit Chopra. As one reads these stories, sometimes the faces of art dealers and the land mafia thriving in metro cities get mixed up. These are tales originating in the tragic, obscene and stinking worlds populated by both the successful artists and the failed unfortunates committing seppuku driven by the trickeries of the art world's cruel colonisers.

Oftentimes one comes up with this feeling that it's the first Hindi novel to articulate the tragedies of artists from small-town India who end up as victims of the conspiracies and competition among art gallery owners and cruel agents. Yet it is marked by its own characteristic and quite original comicality laced with obscenities and eroticism. It's not all that easy to create such a work as the scholarly critics would have us believe.

In the 1970s, John Berger had published a book titled *The Success and Failure of Picasso*, which spelled out in detail the disturbing truths hidden behind the success of great artists. It demolished many a myth about an artist's larger-than-life persona of greatness. One learnt from this book that the great Picasso's notorious genius-like eccentricities or idiosyncrasies were merely deceitful and clever marketing strategies. Berger's this very book also gave currency to the phrase 'methodical madness'. Similarly, if you look at *Seppuku* through the eyes of an economist cum aesthete, it turns out to be in the same mould as a Milton Friedman and *Washington Consensus*, a book retelling the rousing and spicy stories gravitating around the glamorous Page Three but also exciting, poignant, tragic and dark universe of the filthy rich originating in the leftovers and scum of the global corporate market. Quite *sui generis* in Hindi. In it every artist is to be seen in the art bazaar with his own characteristic idiosyncrasy and tricks, eccentricity and cleverness.

The pace at which the narrative of *Seppuku* flows imposes on the reader the pressure to keep up with it. The novel can be read virtually in a jiffy. But later, as one reflects on the core of the narrative, one gets a jolt. *Seppuku*'s central and basic theme leaves one astonished. One wonders if any critic took note of it. Perhaps because Vinod Bhardwaj was constantly alert and, in the style of a master craftsman, managed to keep it hidden behind the novel's outward linguistic recitation and its architecture as evident on the surface. The truth behind the relationship between the market and the artist which he looks keen to convey through the novel is actually constantly camouflaged by him.

The unaimed-for central truth of *Seppuku* is the same well-known truth of economy and commerce where a fake coin always manages to keep the real one out of the market and exchange house—where the copy displaces the original. The point where *Seppuku* concludes is also stunning. It does not conclude in the absurd or surreal Kafkaesque style, but rather indicates the murder of an original work and a sincere artist by a reproduction or a duplicate. And that indeed is the bitter truth of every market. It is not a coincidence that after going through *Seppuku* one suddenly recalls 20th century's great thinker-critic Walter Benjamin's essay 'The Work of Art in the Age of Mechanical Reproduction' in his famous book *Illuminations*. One is surprised at how the truth about today's seppuku was divined so many decades ago by a genius critic of the Hitler-era Germany.

It is believed that the history of *Mona Lisa* is nothing but the sum total of all the uncountable copies and reproductions continuously churned out through the medium of every technique there was between the 17th and the 20th centuries. Indeed the reproduction and the copy are what create the history of the original. Imagine the time when the woodcut made the first assault on the originality of an artwork. How dreadful has the technology made it by our times.

What looks the most resplendent in the market today is not the original but merely the duplicate. The original will not sell because it cannot reproduce itself. The original is what cannot be reborn.

Seppuku also needs to have a postscript, a sort of post-mortem of the art bazaar. If *Seppuku* gets published in English as well then, recalling *Caligula*, Vinod Bhardwaj should weave into it the aphrodisiacal imagery and impressions of the final decline of the Roman Empire. We shall wait.

—**Uday Prakash**

Uday Prakash is considered to be one of the best living Hindi writers of our time. His The Girl with the Golden Parasol *and* The Walls of Delhi *have been published to great acclaim in English. This piece was originally published in Hindi in* Jansatta.